Transported

My Story.

Transported

The Diary of
Elizabeth Harvey, Australia 1790

By Goldie Alexander

■SCHOLASTIC

While the events described and some of the characters in this book may be based on actual historical events and real people, Elizabeth Harvey is a fictional character, created by the author, and her diary is a work of fiction.

Scholastic Children's Books
Commonwealth House, 1–19 New Oxford Street,
London, WC1A 1NU, UK
A division of Scholastic Ltd
London ~ New York ~ Toronto ~ Sydney ~ Auckland
Mexico City ~ New Delhi ~ Hong Kong

First published in Australia by Scholastic Press, 2000
Published in the UK by Scholastic Ltd, 2002

Typeset by TW Typesetting, Midsomer Norton, Somerset
Printed by Mackays of Chatham plc, Chatham, Kent
Cover images: A direct north general view of Sydney Cove, 1794 by Thomas Watling (1762-1814) (after) Dixson Galleries, State Library of New South Wales/Bridgeman Art Library.
The Water girl (oil on canvas) by Victor Thirion (1833-78) Private Collection/Christie's Images/Bridgeman Art Library.

2 4 6 8 10 9 7 5 3 1

Rose Hill

Saturday, 3rd April 1790

Yesterday was Good Friday. Master Henry Dodd gathered his servants together to read "The Lord's Prayer". He made us repeat it after him. Sarah says to never tell anyone that I know my letters. She fears that if the officers hear that I can read and write, they might decide to use me elsewhere, and that this would separate us.

But this morning just after sunrise I was doing the usual house dusting and sweeping when I heard someone say, "My life for one of those cabbages."

My heart leapt into my mouth. Sydney Cove is full of murderers and thieves. What if one had come as far as Rose Hill? Holding my broom as a weapon, I tiptoed into the next room. A young Royal Marine was peering out at our garden. This book was under his arm. Catching sight of me, he blushed to the roots of his hair. Then he introduced himself as Winston Russell and told me that he was here to see Master Dodd.

I took a deep breath and said, "Excuse me, sir. That

book. Is it something you can write in?"

"Why, yes," he said. "This is a journal."

I bobbed a curtsey and tried not to show my excitement. *My life for one of those cabbages.* In this colony, food is power. I knew that I could trade food for just about anything. "Sir," I said, "I could not help overhearing..." He reddened even further. "Could you think of exchanging that journal for a vegetable?"

He licked his lips as if tasting it already. "Maybe for carrots. A cabbage would be nice."

I said, "Would an onion do?"

He shook his head. "My sister Emily is sick. She pines for something fresh. Surely this book is worth three."

That journal! I could not take my eyes off it. In my mind I could touch the clean smooth paper and smell the leathery cover. But this harsh life as a convict has taught me to strike a hard bargain. I said quickly, "I have only two."

"Three," he insisted.

"Two." I turned to leave.

"D—Done," he stammered as I reached the door.

Before he could change his mind, I ran outside to where Old Tom, Master Dodd's chief gardener, has planted rows of onions, carrots, potatoes, turnips and cabbages. I knew what a risk I was taking. Governor Phillip has told Master Dodd to punish any person caught stealing food. If someone saw me, I would get a hundred lashes and be sent back to Sydney Cove.

But for once my luck was in. No one was about. Stepping onto the bed, I pulled out two onions, hid them in my skirt and ran back into the house. The Marine held out his hand, the fingers long and delicate as any girl's, and went to take the onions. I held them behind me and told him to first give me the book.

The corners of his mouth pulled tight, he carefully tore out some pages with writing on them. Saying that I would need ink with which to write, he handed me a small bottle. Only then did we make the exchange.

Before hiding the onions inside his jacket, he held them to his nose as if they were the rarest East Indies spice.

The sun has gone down and I have no candle. These southern skies are so vast. They make me dizzy just to look at them. Now the crickets are starting up. Their song almost deafens me.

Tuesday, 6th April

A fine warm day. All morning I helped Sarah launder our Master's shirts and drape them over the bushes to dry. His poor shirts are so threadbare from too much wear – and too much soaking in hot water and lye – that they are almost transparent. Then back into the house to simmer a mutton shank and some wild spinach for our dinners. Sarah had intended for me to mend shirts until sunset. But as my hands are too red and puffy from washing to thread the needle, she has given me the afternoon to myself.

First I must finish recording last Saturday's events. After I gave the Marine his onions, I held this book to my chest and prayed for him to leave. The longer he stayed, the more trouble I could be in. But he had come with a message for Master Dodd, and see him he would. Settling into a chair whilst assuring me that no word of this business would pass his lips, he said, "D–Did you not sail on the *Lady Penrhyn*?"

I was not surprised that he knew my face. So few of us sailed to Botany Bay, everyone here seems familiar.

He wanted to know why I was so interested in books. I told him that it was not so much books as paper to write on. He paused to consider this. Then, "What is your name, child?"

Child? I thought indignantly. From someone with skin as smooth as a baby's bottom? I bit my lip and stared at our feet – his, in shabby holed boots, and mine, so bare and dusty. His eyes followed my gaze and I felt his shock at glimpsing my scarred toes. He demanded to know how this had happened. I told him the gaolers in Portsmouth had asked for money. When I did not have any, they had promised me a lesson I would never forget.

"Most memorable," was his dry response. Then once again he asked me for my name. I did not know what to do. My first thought was – what if he is caught carrying those onions? Might he not betray me? Then I considered how far he had gone to help his sister. To have risked so much for a loved one must show a kind heart. So I told him that I was Elizabeth Harvey. Then added that folk around here know me as Lizzie.

He leant back in his chair, and this gave me time to look him over. Gingery curls fall onto his collar, and his eyebrows are so thick, they remind me of smudges of orange paint. He is short and slim with fair freckled skin, and his nose is crooked, as if he has been in one fight too many. He said, "Lizzie, why were you sent to Botany Bay?"

"They said I stole a linen gown and a straw bonnet worth seven shillings."

"A very bad crime indeed..."

"But it was not me who did it," I cried now wishing that I had kept my mouth shut.

His gaze was disbelieving. "No convict ever admits her guilt."

"Since I am transported," I cried indignantly, "why must I bother to lie? And it is only a crime for those who do not have to steal to stay alive."

I flushed and fell silent. Rudeness to a marine could bring me a flogging. I waited for him to dismiss me. Instead he said, "Where are you from?"

"Cranham. A village in the Cotswolds. After my parents died, I was sent to London to find work..."

"So you know how to shape your letters?"

As this is unusual for girls from poor families – some masters claim that too much learning will turn us into bad servants – I told him that our vicar had thought me clever enough to learn.

He said, "But now that I have your onions, won't you be too hungry to write?"

12

"Perchance," I replied. "But as there is no paper left in all of Rose Hill, this book is worth a little hunger."

He leaned forward, his clear gaze seeming to see right through me. "Why is this journal so important?"

I sighed to myself. Nothing for it but the truth. Keeping one eye on the door in case Master Dodd came in, I told him how I had left you, my little brother Edward, in Cranham, and how you would surely wish to know that I was still alive.

If anything, this puzzled the Marine, and he asked me how this book might help. I told him that I plan to use it to describe my present life, and a little of how I came to be here. Then I intend posting it to you, Edward, on the very first vessel sailing home.

By now it was mid-morning and Sarah Burke would be wondering where I was. I bobbed the Marine a curtsy and, praying that Master Dodd would not smell those onions on him, tucked the journal under my shawl, and ran towards the kitchen.

Like the rest of Rose Hill, this room is no more than a hut made of wattle branches lined with mud. There are two tiny glass-less windows. The only furniture is a rough table, several makeshift benches, and a couple of straw pallets piled into a corner. This is where Sarah and I sleep. Large boilers of hot water sit on either side of the hearth. When it rains we must dry our clothes on lines blackened by fumes from the fire. Sarah never allows this fire to go out. In summer this hut is so hot we can hardly breathe.

Sarah is Master Dodd's housekeeper and she rules his servants with an iron rod. Since we found each other in Newgate Prison, she has been my constant friend and protector. While she prepared our Master's dinner of salted pork, dried pease and the end of a cabbage, I showed her the journal.

I had hoped she would be pleased for me. Instead she scowled suspiciously and wanted to know how I had got it. Of course I told her. Then all she could say was, "Why risk a flogging for a book?"

"He won't tell," I sullenly replied. "His sister was sick and he was too hungry to bother with anything else."

She dumped another kettle on the hearth, and cried, "What if someone saw you? What if Master Dodd gets to hear of it?"

"I only bartered my share of the crop…"

"Since when did words feed you better than onions? When food is scarce, nothing else matters. If you steal from here, we all suffer."

She picked up a turnip. I ducked under the table –

this would not be the first time Sarah had thrown something at me in a rage. She said, "And another thing … if you speak to the men you put yourself in danger." She tossed the turnip into the boiling water. "Never walk outside without pulling down your bonnet and covering your chest."

But I saw this as a good morning's work. Winston Russell had risked a flogging to care for his sick sister. And I had found a way of writing to you, my little brother. Though it is four long years since we last were together, you are always in my thoughts. I often dream that you are sleeping beside me as you once did.

Wednesday, 7th April

All morning Sarah had me fetching pails of water from the river. Master Dodd had told her to make his cottage as clean as possible. As this cottage is little more than a hut with a beaten earth floor, and always dusty, this is not easy. Perchance our Master is hoping for another visit from Governor Phillip. Before my

Master settled in Rose Hill, he once worked for the Governor, and they are the best of friends.

Sarah says that the Governor thinks Master Dodd the most trustworthy man in all Port Jackson. Though she also adds that my Master puts too much faith in God – and not enough in hard work – to get us out of our misery. But it seems to me that if all my Master says about God is true, and if God were listening, then our poor lives would not be this sad. Yet I would never dare say this aloud, as surely I would be flogged for blasphemy.

I was coming up from the river, a pail in each hand when Simple Sam jumped out from behind some trees. Eyes rolling like cart wheels, spittle flying everywhere, he cried "Aahh... Come with me."

I got such a fright I nearly dropped both pails. "Not now Sam," I said impatiently. "Can't you see that I am busy?"

Sarah says that I should look out for Simple Sam and not let him come too close. But I know that Sam just wants to play – though playing is difficult in that he has a man's face and body, but speaks and thinks like a baby.

Sam's story is as sad a tale as I have ever heard. Once he was a clever villain and counterfeiter. But one day he got careless enough for the London police, the Runners, to catch him and take him to Newgate Prison. There, the gaolers thumped him so hard he ended up a half-wit.

Today his face was almost hidden by a tangled beard and shaggy mane of black hair. Scum dribbled from his nose and there was more dirt on him than you would find in a clay pit. The other convicts tease him unmercifully. They steal his food and rum, and never let him sleep in their huts. They say he stinks like a weasel.

Today I would have had no problem with Sam except for a couple of women watching from the doorway of one of the huts. They started calling Sam and me names and making certain rude gestures. I let fly with a few names myself. Then setting my cap firmly on my head, I hurried to where Sarah was waiting for the water.

Dearest Edward, it is tiresome living alongside villains, drunks, and idiots. But I suppose I should be grateful that I am still alive.

Thursday, 8th April

We are a long day's walk from Sydney Cove. Any news is slow to arrive. However we now know that the Navy ship *Supply* has sailed into Port Jackson. It came to report that the flagship *Sirius*, which was coming from Cape Town with food and other supplies, has been wrecked on a reef at Norfolk Island.

"Have you anything else to report?" Sarah demanded of the sailor who came to deliver this sad news.

That sailor was half-crazed from drinking too much rum. He laughed so hard we could see his blackened stumps. "Why," he cried, "too much sun has addled Lieutenant Maxwell's brain. He rowed around the harbour for two whole days. We had to send out another boat to rescue him from Middle Head."

Poor man. A wonder he is still alive. Sharks live in those waters, and they make a quick meal of anyone unlucky enough to fall in.

"More like he's mad from lack of food." Sarah threw more wood on the fire. "Was there a service for Good Friday?"

"Surely there was," he said. "The Reverend Doctor Williams held it in the Storehouse. But no one had the strength to pray too loud."

"Was there a goodly attendance?"

His shrug told us that he did not know, and what is more, that he did not care. In this kitchen it is always dusk. Crouching in the shadows, I had hoped the sailor would not notice the mutton bone Sarah had left on the table. To my horror he lunged forward to grab it.

Stealing our food? Though my heart bucketed with fright, I kicked and scratched him like a wild cat. Finally Sarah came to the bone's rescue.

The sailor held his head where she had punched it. "What's up, Missus?"

"Off with you, or take more o' this!" She kicked his leg so hard you could almost hear the bone shatter.

The sailor shrieked loud enough to waken the dead. Then he ran down the hill like the devil himself was chasing him.

We watched him disappear behind a clump of spindly trees. "Thinks he can try anything for a ship's biscuit," she said to me.

I said, "What will happen to those poor folk in Sydney Cove?"

Her grim smile revealed where the gaolers in Newgate had knocked out her front teeth. "Who knows, Lizzie? Even our strongest convicts are too weak to do a day's work. And the land around Sydney Cove isn't worth farming."

I stared into the fire. "Perchance the crops on Garden Island will grow enough to feed those folk."

She snorted and went on preparing the Master's dinner. "Anything planted on Garden Island is already stolen. You and me, we're best off at Rose Hill where there's something to put in our bellies. Even if we had food to spare, we have no carts to carry it to Sydney Cove." Her scowl grew worse. "Now Missy, you've more to do than stand around gossiping."

But I could tell from her eyes that she is as worried as I am.

Late last night I glimpsed a band of Indians, or "Aborigines" as Master Dodd calls them, lurking further down the hill. When I pointed them out to Sarah, she thought they would probably come to steal our sheep. She thought them savages who did not know right from wrong.

I told her that I would like to ask them why they paint their bodies to look like actors in a theatre pantomime. At this, she laughed very loudly and said,

"Ask away as much as you like. You'll only get nonsense. When we landed at Botany Bay all they did was cry 'Warra, warra'."

I said, "Perhaps that was their way of welcoming us. They seem gentle enough even if they wear no clothes. Has not Governor Phillip made the native, Baneelon, into his own servant?"

"Sure the poor man'll be murdered in his own bed." And she made sure the kitchen door was firmly bolted from the inside.

Friday, 9th April

Old Tom came to warn us to watch out for snakes. He says last night one crept into the hen-yard and stole two chickens. "I seen that thief well enough," he said pointing to his good eye. "A brown monster. Six foot long. Would steal a child easy as a fowl."

Even Sarah shivered and nothing much scares her. Snakes terrify me. Old Tom says that there are hundreds out there. All different shapes and sizes. He has seen some with diamond scales like fish. Others that sit on their tails and pivot around like wooden tops.

During the day there are large jumping ants that carry a most vicious sting. At dusk, mosquito bites raise welts that itch so badly we scratch them into sores.

But to make up for the insects, there are thousands of colourful birds. Most interesting are the parrots. There are flocks of pink, grey and white parrots. White parrots with mustard crests. Black parrots with black and yellow crests. And parrots with red, green, yellow and blue feathers Old Tom calls "Rose Hillers".

I am most amused by a large-beaked dull-feathered bird who laughs whenever he sees me. And some large black and white birds that sing like angels. Also – and if I had not seen this with my own eyes I would find this hard to believe – there are flightless birds almost as big as small ponies that run in flocks through this valley.

We came expecting to find man-eating lions and tigers. Instead this country abounds with "kangaroos" – strange creatures that hop about on strong back legs. Old Tom says the only animals to fear are the snakes as their venom can kill a dog. Also, a certain black spider that builds tunnels in the ground Tom calls "Widdermakers".

Still, everything here is upside down. Instead of leaves, bark drops off the trees. Winter is summer. Spring is autumn. Two years ago when we first settled in Port Jackson, Governor Phillip gathered us together and told us in his quiet way that without caring for our seeds and animals, this colony would never survive. As a result our cattle, sheep and all the poultry are looked after as if they are King George the Third's own property.

Unlike Botany Bay and Port Jackson, the soil at Rose Hill is rich and deep. Late last year we managed to grow a 26-pound cabbage. It is my job to gather wild spinach to make soup. Sarah brews liquorice-flavoured tea from a creeper growing close by. Master Dodd has told Sarah – and he had heard it from the Governor – that this is a sure cure for scurvy.

Last week Sarah and Old Tom went to Sydney Cove to barter vegetables for meat. She came back with a dozen small fish that she rationed out very carefully. "What I would do for some salted mutton or pork," I moaned.

"Barely any left," she said briskly. "And what's left is more maggot than meat. Some of the convicts are sick with starvation."

"Why don't they shoot more game?"

"No shot for the muskets. The men are too weak to trap kangaroos, though some eat possum." She was busy shaping weevily flour into johnny-cakes. "Now all they can do is fish. But with only two rowing boats and a dozen nets, their catch is poor." She went on to explain how each person's ration is two and a half pounds including the fish's head, skin and bone. "Some of the men worry that they will die of starvation if that's all they eat."

I stared at her in amazement. What I would give for more of that sweet white flesh.

Last night I dreamed that I was back in Cranham. I was walking along the track that led to home. In this dream I could see every hedgerow and dandelion. But when I arrived home, who should be there to greet me but Sarah. Edward, you were still a fat baby, and Sarah was holding you in her arms. "Where is Mama?" I asked her.

She smiled at me and said, "Your mama has gone away. I am to be yours and Edward's mama now…"

At this, you burst into loud sobs and woke me up.

When I told Sarah my dream, she held me very close. Then, as if mightily embarrassed, she sent me to check the hen-yard for eggs. Even though she knows the hens are hardly laying.

Saturday, 10th April

We are so busy cleaning the Master's house it is hard to find time to write in my journal. Then this quill made horrid blots and I had to raid the hen-yard for a fresh feather. The cock crowed so loudly, Old Tom came running in. In spite of Tom's scarred face, which could frighten even the bravest heart, he has a soft spot for children. He cast his one good eye over the hens – they were busy scratching up the dust – and said, "Thought I'd catch another of those thieving Indians."

Last week an Aborigine was caught spearing a pig and Old Tom had him severely flogged for it. He later reported that his tribe set up enough crying and wailing to waken the dead.

But Edward, I must ask myself why people are whipped for trying to stay alive? It would seem most strange if they lay down meekly to die of starvation. Not that Governor Phillip would agree. He is determined to deal most severely with anyone caught stealing food.

I later said to Sarah, "What if those Indians think all food is there for the taking?"

She looked at me most oddly. "Why would they think that?"

"Well…" I hesitated. "Someone told Old Tom that the Indians do not keep animals or grow crops. He says that they stay alive through hunting. Whoever catches the animal, why he gets to share it with whoever he chooses."

She sighed impatiently. "Lizzie, you have such queer notions. After all we've been through, I reckon you'd show more sense. And something you should know – Old Tom says someone's been stealing his onions."

My heart nearly stopped beating. "Does he know it was me?"

She placed her hands on her hips. "Why should he?"

"Well…" I paused uncertainly. "Who does he think stole them?"

"An Indian. Or one o' the men. But Lizzie," her voice rose warningly, "promise me no more thieving?"

That I did. But she has accepted that I must, that I will write. Then warns me to do so in private.

Edward, you will want to know what my friend Sarah looks like. She is a big woman, tall and strong with a mop of unruly brown curls that defy any attempt to brush into order. Yesterday she stood over me admiring the way I shape my letters. Though I know that she cannot read these pages, I am careful not to write anything that might annoy her. While I was waiting for this page to dry, she picked it up saying that she could hardly see the marks for looking. Then she told me to mix more charcoal into the ink.

I have offered to teach her the alphabet. But she says she has better things to do than waste her time with learning.

At last a cool breeze wafts over Rose Hill. It reminds me of home. Edward, my stomach aches with loneliness. Sometimes I dream that the bush outside our window has disappeared. I am no longer in this immense land where everything is grey and lonely. Instead I am back in Cranham surrounded by green fields and low stone hedges. Jonquils and daffodils grow in the round green hills beyond our cottage. The air is misty with rain. Holding your small hand in mine, I run to where Mama and Papa wait for us with a warm supper.

Then tears roll down my cheeks as I remember that Mama and Papa are no longer alive. That four long years must pass before we can be together.

Sarah says we must make the best of what we have. Last night for maybe the hundredth time she told me how she was still a baby when her real mother gave her to Mistress Sally Tomkins who ran a home for unwanted children.

This filthy old woman was the closest Sarah ever knew as a mother. She fed Sarah just enough to keep her alive and dressed her in rags. But as soon as Sarah was old enough to walk, she sent her into the streets to pick up whatever she could find. Sometimes it was a gentleman's watch or a purse filled with money. And once a splendid top hat.

"What if you could not find anything?" I asked.

Her gaunt face took on a slow smile. "Then I'd make myself cry so people would throw me pennies."

When I asked Sarah if she ever did meet her own mother, tears ran down her cheeks. To add to her misery, she gave birth to a stillborn boy while we were still in the hulks waiting to be transported. It is a miracle that Sarah is still alive. In prison most of the pregnant women got very sick and died.

She tells me that if God were to bless her with another baby, she would look after it with her last breath. She pretends to be tough as mahogany but she is really very emotional. "Meanwhile," she cries, clutching me to her bony chest, "you, Lizzie, can be my child."

I always hug her back, though she is all ribs and bones. Not at all like our own Mama who was soft and comfortable. Also the few teeth Sarah has left have rotted from the terrible food we had in prison and her breath stinks something terrible. Still, I am lucky to have such a faithful companion – even though sometimes I would wish that she was more my age. It is not that I am ungrateful to Sarah for all she has done for me. If it were not for her, I would now be mad or dead. But Sarah will treat me as a child when I no longer feel like one.

Our early years were so different from hers. Edward, can you recall sitting on Mama's lap while she sewed? I remember pricking myself on her needle. Though Mama scolded me for not being more careful, Papa kissed the spot until it felt better. Another time I remember Mama lying on her bed, her brow damp with sweat. Mistress Bowen from next door shooed me outside, even though it was snowing and fearfully cold.

Then hearing the cry of a newborn baby.

That baby was you. For a long time you were so quiet, we thought you would not live. Mama had already birthed four sons, and all had died. But with the warmer weather, your health picked up. By the time you could sit up by yourself, you were smiling and watching everything I did as if you needed to learn it all.

No more writing. Sarah is calling for more logs for the fire.

Sunday, 11th April

Before prayers Sarah asked me to carry a basket with turnip and potato tops to Mistress Herricks. Also a potion steeped with a clearing oil. Since last winter, the Herricks' elder children have had poor chests. Sarah is anxious to hear if they are spitting blood. If they are, we know their chances are not so good. But Mistress Herricks assured me that the poultice is helping very nicely. Her youngest child, Johnny, is barely six months old. When he sees me, he breaks into a gummy smile. I love to hold him. He is as plump as you used to be, Edward. His little hands and feet are so sweet and unused, they remind me of starfish. Mistress Herricks lives in a hut they share with another family. I saw a dozen straw pallets propped against the walls. Even those that live in the family huts are very cramped.

My Master keeps over a hundred men and women convicts at Rose Hill to help with the crops. But Old Tom has no respect for the men. He says they would not know a cabbage from a monkey. He says that if he did not keep watch, they would pull up every potato plant thinking they were weeds.

Since these are city folk who have never pulled a potato out of the ground, it is hardly surprising. But I would never say this aloud. Old Tom would most likely strike me if I said something he disliked. He can be most unfair. Perchance someone should remind him that last February those same men managed to harvest a little grain and vegetables.

The single men sleep ten to a hut, sometimes even more. The single women are a little more comfortable. But I hate to walk between those huts, as both men and women call rude things, and make rude gestures, to every passer-by.

"Remember to make yourself small," Sarah reminded me before I left.

The day was warm. Still, I wrapped my shawl about me so no one could see that I am starting to become a woman. Not that Sarah is pleased that I am growing up. She insists that I am best off trying to stay a child, and thinks it a good thing that I am only four feet ten.

As I walked, I recalled our first two years in this colony. They have been so hard. Landing at Botany Bay, we found hardly any fresh water, so the Governor decided that we should sail further north to Port Jackson. What followed was eighteen months of sleeping in tents and quarrelling over rations. We were always hungry. Our first crops withered. Many of our animals escaped into the bush or ate poisonous grasses and died. Even the fish would no longer take our baits.

It seemed to Sarah and myself that we would surely die. That is, until the day she heard that Master Dodd was looking for a housekeeper. She went to him saying, "I promise to never steal from you, not even a morsel, were I dying of hunger."

Master Dodd thought it rare to come across such an honest convict. He gave her the job and allowed her to bring to Rose Hill whoever she might choose. And this is how I happen to be here.

I hear her calling. I had best leave this for later.

Wednesday, 14th April

This year we have had hardly any rain, but last night it poured as if the heavens must empty. Today an ocean of mud surrounds us. All the hard work Sarah and I had managed in Master Dodd's house has been undone.

Our Master saw our disappointment and told us not to despair. He assured us that one day we would have a better house that will be easier to clean. It will be built of bricks and mortar, and have proper wooden floors and glass windows and green grass and stone paths leading up to it. Though his grizzled face and voice remained gruff, his eyes twinkled. He added, I think mostly for Sarah's benefit, that it will have a fine set of oak stairs and at least a dozen bedrooms.

I wish that he had not teased her. Now she will not stop complaining how hard it will be to look after so many rooms.

Friday, 16th April

On this side of the equator, this season is autumn. But how can you tell the seasons apart when there is no snow and most days are the same? What we have here is wet and hot. Or dry and hot – though not as hot as it was in February and March.

"If only this was an English spring," I said to Sarah as we spread laundry on bushes to dry.

"Hmmph…" She straightened up to wipe her forehead with the back of her hand. "All I ever knew of spring was melting snow and mud cold enough to freeze the marrow in me bones."

I had to agree that spring in the city is different from spring in the country.

"Spring in the Cotswolds," I said dreamily, "makes me think of wild hares, daffodils and swallows. Big white swans. Foxes and finches and running through grass so green, it hurts my eyes to look at it."

That sent Sarah into gales of laughter. "More like in the city it's warm enough to melt what folk leave in the streets. Spring ain't no blessing if you happen to be poor."

I nodded ruefully. She is right. London is the dirtiest, most foul place in the whole wide world if you are only a servant girl. Though Sydney Cove is not much better.

Sarah threw me another damp sheet to spread over a bush. "Best you get o'er your grieving for Cranham," was her advice.

I have promised myself not to be so homesick. But I have no such control over my sleep. Many nights I dream that I am back home with Mama, Papa and you, Edward, you are still a baby. Suddenly some dread person is knocking on our door. He has come to carry me away...

Saturday, 17th April

Just after sunset I went outside to fetch more wood. You can imagine my fright to see a group of natives watching this house. They can move so quietly, I swear not even an ant would hear them. They stood there observing me. So I stared back. The men had long shaggy hair and beards and wore no clothes. Though their appearance was savage, I felt that if I offered them no threat they would not hurt me.

Several women stood behind the men. Woven baskets were slung over their shoulders and strapped to their waists. Most carried babies. One stepped forward and held out her child for me to admire. He may have been a year old or maybe less. But he was fat and healthy enough, though snot dribbled from his nose into his mouth. His mother pointed to the hen-yard and then to her mouth. Then they chattered between themselves, some laughing and showing off excellent white teeth.

I did not know what to do. If Old Tom thought they had come to steal his poultry he would have them captured and flogged. So I picked up a branch and crashed it about making lots of noise. When I next looked around, every native had vanished.

I wondered very much about them. Some of the women seemed so young. The one carrying the baby could scarcely be older than me. Edward, I could not help wondering what it must be like to never live in a proper house. To speak their strange tongue. To have a baby of my own.

After they had gone, I went back inside and

reported what I saw to Sarah.

She said, "They're no better than animals. Walking around as naked as Adam and Eve."

"Some of the women on the *Lady Penrhyn* went around with little more," I reminded her.

"They were no better than animals too," was her reply. "Just as unnatural."

But Edward, I think that this is different. These natives act as if wearing clothes is unnatural rather than the other way around. It is all very strange.

Sunday, 18th April

After prayers I spent all day darning and patching. Master Dodd is impressed with the neatness of my stitches. He demanded to know where I had learned to sew so well. I told him that our mama had shown me. I wish I could tell him that I can also read and write. But Sarah is so against this, I just do not dare. Sarah has just shown me where I missed a small tear in a pillow casing. If I do not patch it right away, she threatens me that feathers other than these will fly.

Monday, 19th April

I have two rescues to report. The first was mine. A log fell out of the fire and I burned myself trying to push it back. Sarah plunged my hand into a pail of water. Now my hand hurts. But it is only red and not blistered.

The second rescue is far more interesting. After I burned my hand Sarah said I would only be a nuisance in her kitchen. Instead she sent me to the river to report on what is happening there.

I reminded her that she tells me to always stay away from places where men gather.

She said that this time was different as the convicts are supposed to be cutting more reeds to thatch our roofs. These thatches are woven in the same way as at home. Rats love to live in them, as do some small black and brown beetles Old Tom calls roaches.

I was running across a bushy patch of ground when I heard someone cry out for help

Without worrying about my own safety, I raced towards the voice. Who should I find but a small girl? She was maybe five years of age, and by her gentle appearance, certainly not a convict's child.

Simple Sam had his arms around her, and she was screaming with terror.

"Away with you, Sam," I cried and he fled into the bush while I helped the poor thing to her feet.

She was crying fit to burst. Tears poured from her eyes and nose. She pointed to her ankle which swelled even as I looked at it. Between more bouts of tears, she told me that she had been searching for her papa. Thinking he was by the river she had taken a short cut through the bush. Then she had tripped and lain there, too winded and sore to move.

This was how Sam found her. I think that he has no true evil in him, and that he was only trying to help her back onto her feet. But seeing those loopy eyes and hearing his strange speech, she was so frightened she started to scream.

"Hush now," I said firmly for how else should one treat a wrought-up child, even one this fair and delicate? Then I held her as close as I would hold you, Edward, when you were upset. Soon the worst of her sobbing eased, though her chest still heaved with fright and pain.

Now I could think more clearly, I said, "Where are your mama and papa?"

She pointed towards the barracks. I picked her up (she was light as a feather) and very slowly piggybacked her to the barracks.

A Marine must have seen us coming and warned her papa, for he came rushing out to meet us.

Taking no more notice of me than if I were a horse or a dog, he picked up the child and rushed her inside. At first I was sad that he did not even bother to thank me for rescuing his child. But then I thought how his concern showed that he must be a very caring papa indeed.

I went into the kitchen to tell Sarah all about it. She said, "Did you expect him to give you a reward?"

I shook my head. "The little girl was very frightened. Maybe even frightened enough to cause an injury."

Sarah raised herself from where she was crouched over a pan of vegetable peelings and rubbed her aching back. "Your trouble, Lizzie," she said firmly, "is that you think you're good as gentry. You're only a convict girl and don't you ever forget it."

Edward, I must accept this. Though for some reason – even though it is four years since I last saw Cranham – it still pains me each time I think of it.

Tuesday, 20th April

Tonight Sarah filled a cauldron with warm water. We took turns sitting in it. I wallowed in the water like a fish. Using a milk ladle, I poured water over my hair to rid it of dust and knots. It feels good to wash myself all over. In prison I was so lice-ridden and dirty, I swear that if our poor mama had been alive, she would not have recognized me. In the eight and a half months we sailed on the *Lady Penrhyn*, the only washing we knew was during a storm when the sea came flooding into the night-dungeons.

"I would as rather be dead than as dirty as we once were," I said to Sarah.

"Would you now?" She chuckled. "What if you have no kettle?"

I laughed back. "There is always the river."

"Too cold for me," she cried, her smile vanishing. Ever since she nearly fell overboard during a storm sailing out from Cape Town, she has had a deep fear of water.

We dried ourselves on the ends of an old sheet, and

I brushed my hair using the back of a metal pan as a mirror. All the time we were on board, I never saw my own reflection. Even now this face that looks back at me seems unfamiliar. Sarah says it is changing because I am growing into a woman.

"You'd have pretty pink round cheeks if you got enough to eat," she said watching me untangle my hair. "And a decent kind of nose." She stared at me thoughtfully. "Also, your eyes are the same blue as calm waters. But you need to grow more."

"One day I will," I insisted. "Mama and Papa were not so short."

"Maybe you will." But her tone was doubtful. And as we settled ourselves on our pallets, she went on to talk about other things.

Sleep comes slowly where there are flying beetles, mosquitoes, river rats and possums (squirrel-like furry creatures with wet noses and long tails) racing across the roof. Still, I felt better for losing all that dirt.

Sarah has given me a tiny piece of candle all my very own to write by.

Wednesday, 21st April

All my bathing was undone this morning when Old Tom asked me to rake out the pig-pen. Because Old Tom knows our papa was a farmer, he likes me to help with country tasks.

Raking away stinky pig droppings is not to my liking, and I loudly sent all pigs to the devil. A large black and pink sow glared evilly back. To add to my dislike, Old Tom told me Governor Phillip had planned to send those very pigs into the bush to increase their numbers.

I paused in my raking. "Why didn't he?"

Tom's one good eye winked at me. "Wouldn't those darned Indians eat every one?"

I have been waiting for him to tell me that someone had stolen two onions. So far he has said nothing. Perchance he has decided to forget them.

Mid-day, Sarah and I had settled down to scraps of salt-meat stewed with turnip tops when Uriah Small came to tell me to go to the barracks.

Uriah lives in one of the family huts with his mother

and brother. Hair spills over his eyes so he can hardly see and his face is covered in grime. When I asked him who was calling for me, he said, "Surgeon asks to talk with you," and took off down the muddy track that leads to the barracks.

I settled my cap, wrapped myself in a shawl and hurried to catch up. "Many surgeons sailed with us from Portsmouth," I said to him. "Which one is it?"

He mumbled something under his breath and raced ahead. When we got to the barracks, he ran inside. I was too scared to follow. Has not Sarah always warned me to stay away from where men gather?

I drew figures in the dust with my toes. Soon a man emerged from the barracks. He came over to where I stood, and I recognized him as the papa of the child I had rescued. Tall and with a military bearing, I think that he must have once been quite stout because his jacket hung on him like a scarecrow's. His complexion was leathery from too much sun, his red hair flecked with grey, his eyes steel blue, and his square chin covered in reddish stubble.

I bobbed a curtsey and waited for him to speak. He looked me up and down. "Are you the convict Elizabeth Harvey?"

"Yes, sir," I said. How did he know my name?

The gentleman chewed his lower lip awhile. "Do you know who I am?"

"No, sir." I shook my head. Then it came to me in a rush. Those onions! Wretched Winston Russell must have confessed. I was as good as dead. Strong men could barely survive a hundred lashes. Much less someone as small and weak as I am.

He said, "Surgeon James Russell, at your service."

Winston Russell's father! Again I nearly fainted. Only this time with relief.

The Surgeon was saying "...wish to thank you on two counts. Firstly for saving my daughter..." He shuddered slightly. "This last year in Port Jackson, already two small girls have been attacked."

I pulled myself together. Someone must defend poor Sam or for certain he would be flogged. "Sam is stupid," I cried. "That is why he is called Simple Sam. But there is no harm in him. He was only trying to help the little girl back onto her feet..."

"Possibly you are right." But his shrug was unconvinced. "As for that other business with my son..." He cleared his throat behind his hand. "Best if that is quickly forgotten."

Just then the little girl limped out from the barracks. Now she was no longer crying, I could see that she was as pale skinned as her father and brother. But where they have gingery hair, hers is almost white. She has pale grey eyes, and the most dainty arms and legs I have ever seen. She is so delicate, she reminds me of a china figurine.

"This is Emily," her father told me. "As you can see, she has a badly sprained ankle."

I glanced down. Sure enough, a rag was tightly wrapped around her right leg.

Her papa said, "My children lost their mother at sea. Now I must be both mother and father to them." He stood back to consider me. "Where are your parents?"

My eyes filled with tears. "Sir, all I have in the world is one brother, and I was forced to leave him in Cranham."

"Cranham," he mused. "Where might that be?"

"Sir, the Cotswolds in the west of England."

Dearest Edward, as soon as this came out of my mouth, I had a sudden vision of soft green hills and misty rain. Homesickness leaves an ache in my stomach that I am sure no surgeon, no matter how clever he might be, can ever cure.

The Surgeon said, "Elizabeth Harvey, how old are you?"

"Thirteen, sir. And most folk call me Lizzie."

"Lizzie," he murmured sounding my name so sweetly I hardly recognized it. "Lizzie … Lizzie … Lizzie." To my surprise his mouth turned down as if recalling something sad. Then he sighed and said more sternly, "Lizzie, you must be very wicked to be brought here. You are very young to be transported."

I kept my gaze on the ground. I would have liked to tell him that the judge who sentenced me to seven years in Botany Bay did not think that I was too young. But it is said that the Old Bailey judges sup every night with the devil.

He mused, "Perhaps you are better off in Sydney Cove. London is full of children crippled by those who should care for them."

I nodded, not quite agreeing about things being so much better here. But Edward, in the two years I lived in the city, I had seen such wickedness: children apprenticed to men and women and used so cruelly, they would be crippled for the rest of their days. Others who would die of cold and starvation if it were not for what they managed to steal.

I waited for Surgeon Russell to say why he had sent for me. He still seemed to be thinking aloud. "Dean Jonathan Swift offers an interesting solution to dealing with unwanted children."

"What would that be, sir?" I asked, hoping that he would not mind me asking.

Surgeon Russell cocked his head to one side. "Why, in a tract he calls 'A Modest Proposal' he suggests that we farm our poorest children as meat."

I stared at him in horror. Could these men be serious?

The Surgeon smiled grimly. "I think this is mostly to bring the problem to our government's attention. Grave problems deserve grave answers." Recalling why I had been brought to him, he said briskly, "You should know that I intend to ask Mister Dodd to release you from his service. I need someone to care for Emily. She must have someone with her night and day. My medical duties take me away too often. Also," he frowned a little, "Winston tells me that you can read and write. If we had stayed in Sydney Cove, Emily was to attend a school run by Isabella Rosson – a good woman though she is a convict."

While we were talking, a platoon of solders in grubby red coats and white trousers emerged from the barracks. They gradually moved into two lines. One soldier beat a drum. Another played a merry tune on a fife. The drill sergeant shouted, "Left, right, left, right. Eyes ... right!" Soldiers marched up and down.

Surgeon Russell's voice rose over the noise. "While

we are in Rose Hill, Emily must not neglect her lessons. I will ask you to read with her every day for one hour and to see that she practises her letters."

Taking in my bewildered face, he nodded lightly, and stalked back inside.

I turned to Emily who merely giggled. She popped me a curtsy and limped after her papa. They left me as gawky-eyed and amazed as poor Simple Sam himself.

Eventually I pulled myself together and returned to Sarah's kitchen. There, I repeated the conversation as well as I could remember it. To Sarah's credit she made it seem as if she was delighted at my change of fortune. But I could see that she was upset at being separated from me.

"Never mind, Sarah," I cried. "I will sleep with you every night."

"I doubt it," she said tartly. "The Surgeon won't want his daughter sleeping here. He'll expect you to stay with her night and day, won't he?"

"I suppose you are right," I said wistfully, for this will be the first time in two years that we have been apart. "But I will visit you every day," I promised and though she growled that it would make little difference to her – and that she had far too much to do than to bother with visitors – she seemed a little happier.

Thursday, 22nd April

Uriah returned this morning to tell me to move my belongings to one of the larger family huts about a hundred yards down the track.

Sarah watched me collect my linsey-woolsey petticoat, my cotton shift, my two cotton stockings and my woollen jacket. All are sadly frayed. Then this quill, a bottle filled to the top with ink and my most precious diary. These few possessions I stowed inside the raggedy sheet we used to dry ourselves on the other night.

Sarah hated to see me go. At the last minute she placed one of her own precious caps in my package, saying that mine was too shabby to be respectable. She reminded me how I must always keep away from places where men gather and to be prudent where I went and with whom I spoke. She finished off with, "If you venture out of the hut after dusk by yourself, then surely you'll be sorry."

I promised her to be extra careful now she was no longer around to protect me. We hugged and kissed, both weeping at being separated. I said that I would return as soon as I could. But she thought that I would have little time for visiting.

Mindful of her warnings, I walked past the huts where the convict men live. They greeted me with the usual bad language and gestures. I gazed straight ahead and pretended to be deaf.

When I reached the Russell's hut, both the Surgeon and Emily were waiting to greet me. Surgeon Russell took me aside to say very gravely, "My daughter Emily suffers from a weak heart and extreme shortness of breath. She could die if she over exerts herself. It is your task to keep her as quiet as possible. You understand?"

I told him that I did. Then telling me that he had many duties to attend to, but that he would be back before dusk, he hurried away.

Emily showed her delight by constant chatter. She showed me all her clothes and her toys. She has managed to bring with her a wooden hobbyhorse and a cloth doll. That poor thing was sadly in need of stitching. I promised her that if she was good and learned her lessons very quickly, that I would fix this doll and maybe sew her another.

I can see that she is very excitable. Edward, it will

be a great effort on my part to keep her as quiet as her papa insists.

So far things go well. The Surgeon seems kind, if a little absentminded. But when he is home I keep out of his way. I must not do anything to irritate him. A convict's existence can be so unfair. Long ago I learned that a master has total power. Even if he is the gentlest of souls, he can make my life a misery.

Friday, 23rd April

Edward, I must describe my new home for you. This hut is little different from the others, though perhaps slightly wider. The walls are twigs plastered with mud. The roof is a thatch woven from reeds. The floor is hard packed earth. If a fire came through, all that might survive is the stone hearth.

The Surgeon's family sleeps on straw pallets no better than us convicts. During the day we pile these pallets into a corner. Like all the other huts in Rose Hill and Sydney Cove, we are plagued with rats and biting insects. Possums nest in the thatched roof. They sleep during the day and look for food only at night. Our furniture is a rough table and some benches. I have two large boilers or cauldrons for heating water and cooking.

As for my duties: Surgeon Russell expects me to collect water and firewood, cook, clean, wash, care for Emily and supervise her lessons. I shall scarcely find time to catch my breath. Still, I am better off than many others. I have a roof over my head, a kind Master, a pretty young charge to care for, and a little food to fill the empty space in my belly.

Emily has few clothes, but what she shows me has been lovingly worked. Seems that her mama did all this fine embroidery. She says that though her mama is dead, that she keeps watch on both her children from Heaven.

Winston has yet to appear. Emily says he is sleeping in the barracks with the other Marines. She assures me that he knows that I am now part of their household. I wonder what he makes of this?

I asked Emily why they left Sydney Cove. She says that her papa had been commanded by the Governor to bring certain messages to Master Dodd. After packing their belongings, the Surgeon hired a soldier's horse to bring them to Rose Hill. "And your brother, Winston?" I asked. "Was he too, given permission?"

Emily's gaze was unblinking. "Papa asked the Governor if he could come with us. The Governor said he could help Papa deliver his messages."

"Oh." I tried not to look curious. "How did you happen to sail to Botany Bay?"

"Oh, Winston had always wished to be a Marine. Then Papa said that as we had lost all our money, that now he must be a ship's Surgeon."

"Was your mama pleased?"

"She didn't say," the child said gravely. "But I heard her crying when she thought Papa wouldn't hear."

Last night, as we sat over our small supper, my new Master told me that he is a great believer in certain vegetables and herbs as a cure for many illnesses.

I would have liked to question him further, but he seems to expect silence. If Emily chatters too much he can be quite curt with her. If I irritate him, he might send me away.

Saturday, 24th April

I cannot believe how busy I am. Every waking minute seems filled with a new task that cannot wait until tomorrow.

Emily's lessons have started well. This morning we drew letters in the dust. She can easily tell A's from C's. But she has trouble distinguishing D's from B's. When she started to cry, I assured her that tomorrow she would do better.

Hardtack and pease pudding for dinner. I saved some for tomorrow. I must, I will, find time to visit Sarah. Perchance she can persuade Old Tom to part with a few vegetables. Also, I am sure Emily would do well if she ate wild spinach. This vegetable will bring colour into her cheeks. I know where this grows. Tomorrow I will go to this place and fill a basket.

Winston turned up this morning. He pretended to Emily that we had never met. He is polite, though not at all friendly. I am always mindful that he is a soldier and thus my gaoler. But I like the way he occupies Emily without tiring her. They sit on the floor and play knuckles. With me he is always guarded. He never discloses much about himself or what he is thinking.

Earlier on, I overheard a conversation between them that saddened me more than I can say. Emily had asked Winston if he was as fond of me as she is.

"As much as I can be," he dryly answered. Then he added, "Emily do not get too attached to Lizzie. She is a convict and has been sent here for a crime. Whether she admits to b–being guilty or not."

In spite of his distrust, or maybe because of it, I later plucked up courage to ask him how he spent his time in the barracks.

He raised those thick orange eyebrows as if surprised at my question. "Why, we march up and d–down."

"Is that all you do?"

He reddened. "Some of our soldiers find this life most tedious. They drink too much rum and gamble. While some grow rich, others lose everything they own."

"But there is so much to do in Rose Hill," I cried. "Why don't they help us plough the fields for the next planting? Why not help us make bricks and build proper houses?"

Winston looked so shocked I could hardly suppress a giggle. "We are soldiers, not servants," he said indignantly. "Our only task is to mind you convicts, not toil in the fields."

It was on the tip of my tongue to retort that they have not always been too successful at this. Several convicts have run away to China. Some were lost forever. Others returned and were whipped for trying to escape. One unfortunate man met a native's spear instead of freedom.

Whenever Winston talks to me, his stammer grows worse. I can only think this is because he dislikes me so much. But it is best that I do not antagonize him. Best that we remain on good terms when I am a convict and he is my gaoler.

After we had eaten and were sitting quietly looking into the fire, he said, "Lizzie, I find it strange that a farmer's daughter speaks like she is gentry. Though the soft way you pronounce your A's tells me that you are not a Londoner. Also your round face and turned up nose are most unusual." When my eyes widened, he said impatiently, "Surely you have noticed how alike all London sparrows look? All have pale skins, pinched features and bandy legs."

I decided to ignore his comments on my appearance. "Mama insisted that we never sound like country folk. So did Doctor Nelson."

He raised an inquiring eyebrow.

"Doctor Nelson was our parson," I explained. "He taught me how to write my letters." I went on to tell him how this good man had encouraged me to read the Bible. And how he owned a book called *The Whole Life and Merry Exploits of Bold Robin Hood*. Hard to remember that I was once that small child so enthralled by Robin Hood's adventures.

"Why, I know that book very well," he cried. "And there is another called *The Adventures of Robinson Crusoe* by Daniel Defoe that is even more exciting."

"What is that about?"

"Nothing more than one man doing the same as us. Robinson Crusoe is shipwrecked on a desert island."

"Is he always alone?"

"After some years he meets a native he baptizes Man Friday…" He broke off as if recalling that we must not get too friendly.

I stared pensively into the fire. I have tried to harden myself against him and not to let him hurt my feelings. But given these strange surroundings, I very much wanted to know if Robinson Crusoe had managed any better than us.

I stirred myself enough to ask why Crusoe did not die of starvation. Winston told me that in the beginning Crusoe was very hungry as he had no musket. Only he taught himself to trap animals and fish. Also, he planted vegetables and looked for plants that were safe to eat.

"Which is more than we do here," I said tartly.

Of course Winston thought by *we*, I meant *him*. He immediately took offence and this brought the conversation to an abrupt end.

Sunday, 25th April

As Emily's ankle is so much better, hardly swollen at all, I said that she might come with me to a bend in the river where the men are rarely seen.

I had already noticed how she loves any activity. She likes nothing better than to skip, hop and jump. I must constantly remind her to stay quiet. Sometimes I think that she is more a nymph or maybe a sprite, and it will be hard to follow her papa's instructions.

Halfway through the morning I packed some leftover pease porridge into a wicker basket and we set off. Though the day was overcast, the sun kept trying to break through. Mindful of Emily's complexion, I insisted that she put on her bonnet. At first she refused and I had to convince her that the sun would burn her cheeks strawberry-red.

All the way she chattered like a starling. I soon learned that the family had travelled by coach from Cornwall. After waiting in Portsmouth, they had sailed to Botany Bay on the storeship, *Golden Grove*. There were no convicts on this ship, so Emily was saved from witnessing the terrible things that happened on the *Lady Penrhyn*.

When I asked her how it happened that her mama went to Heaven, tears welled up in her eyes. She said, "Not just Mama. Also my baby brother. Now Mama and Baby are together."

I mopped her tears with my petticoat. "But you still have your papa and Winston. I left my brother Edward in England when he was the same age as you are now. These days I have only Sarah to care for me."

"Lizzie, *I* care for you," she stoutly insisted. "You are my very best friend, except for Papa and Winston. Who is Sarah?"

"Sarah is my friend and protector. You will meet her very soon."

She looked at me with eyes pale as new milk. "Will Sarah like me?"

I assured her that Sarah would love her, but only if she worked hard at learning her letters and always stayed quiet. All this time we had been walking along a bushy track flanked by trees with stringy bark like an old man's skin. Further along were curious low black stumps sprouting greenish-grey fronds like horsetails.

When we came to my favourite spot along the river, I seated myself on a fallen log, and pulled her down beside me. We dangled our toes in the water. The air was filled with the bittersweet scent of decaying bark. Trees met their reflection in brownish water and dragonflies skimmed across the surface. It was so peaceful, for a moment I almost forgot to pine for home.

Suddenly a fearful crashing broke out. Heart hammering in my ears, I sprang to my feet and wrapped my arms around Emily. It sounded as if a herd of stampeding horses, or maybe wild boars, was heading our way. An angry boar can be more dangerous than even a dragon. We shivered and clung to each other. Wherever I looked, shadowy groves hid one-eyed monsters that I knew were only waiting to spring out at us.

Then Emily pointed to the other side of the river. Crashing about in the undergrowth were two kangaroos. These animals were using their short front paws to box each other.

Safe on the opposite bank, we asked them why they were fighting. The kangaroos took no notice of us whatsoever. In a few minutes they – and any monsters that might be around – vanished into the forest.

We settled back to our puddings. Just as I was brushing crumbs off Emily's pinafore, I felt someone come up from behind. I swivelled around to see the native girl I had seen before. She was carrying a baby and this time she was alone. As we stood facing each other, she reached towards Emily. I saw her finger touch Emily's pale arm and I marvelled at the contrast.

I think that the native girl had never seen such white skin. She said something that sounded like "Iora, iora," and pointed to herself.

I assured her that we would very much like to be her friend. If she did not understand my words, she felt my tone, and she held out her baby for us to admire. As he was entirely naked I could see that he was fat and healthy. He would have been most appealing except for his snotty nose.

I went to wipe it away. The girl took fright. Next

minute she and the baby had melted back into the bush.

Emily was deeply disappointed. She cried, "Why did she go? I so much wanted to play with her baby."

Tuesday, 27th April

This morning it was too windy and dust-blown to hang the washing over the bushes. Perhaps this is a good thing because we are almost out of soap. The food situation is worse. We are given only a handful of rice and a tiny piece of salt pork a day – hardly enough for each person to manage two mouthfuls.

It seemed as good a time as any to take Emily to visit Sarah. But first I had to ask her papa for permission. He chewed his lip as he considered my request. Then he said, "Lizzie, I am well pleased with you. You are proving yourself a fine servant."

I felt my face redden. Praise from this new Master is praise indeed.

He said, "Is not your friend Sarah Burke housekeeper to Master Dodd?"

I nodded.

"Then certainly you may visit her. But, you must never let Emily out of your sight. Not even for a second. And you must make sure that she never gets tired."

"If she walks, I will see that she does so very slowly," I promised. "And when she tires, I will piggyback her."

Emily and I set off shortly after. I worried about walking the track between the men and women's huts. To my relief, hardly anyone was about, as their language would make a grown man blush.

Emily wanted to know what games I played when I was little. So I told her about raiding blackbird and finch nests, and how I liked to hold the eggs in my hand. She listened very intently. "What colour were they?"

"Pale blue. Sometimes speckled white."

"Did not the birds mind you taking their eggs?"

"Perchance they did. Sometimes the bird was nesting. I remember how they would look up at me in fright."

She wanted to know what else we did. So I told her spinning tops, tag, and chasing each other around the meadow and the same knucklebones she played with Winston, and sometimes hoops.

By now we had reached Master Dodd's kitchen. Sarah came out at the sound of our voices and nodded at me as if I had been gone less than an hour. I introduced Emily, who bobbed a curtsey. Sarah smiled and I could see that she thought Emily as sweet and pretty as I do.

We stayed half the day. When Emily was not listening, I managed to tell Sarah about the child's frail condition. "Why, the poor little thing," Sarah cried. "We must build up her strength."

She boiled wild spinach and two potatoes each for our dinners. Before we started I was mindful to loudly thank God for this tasty meal. (Emily's papa has urged me to pray before each meal, but I wonder, can He be listening?) Then we savoured those vegetables as if they were the most splendid banquet set before King George.

Before we left, Sarah mentioned that the cow was in calf and giving a little milk. She poured some into a tin cup and told Emily to drink it up, as it would stop her getting weak bones and bandy legs.

Emily's pale gaze turned to me. She said, "Lizzie's legs are straight." So I told her that was because our mama owned a milk-cow called Daisy who gave us plentiful butter and cream.

Also Sarah slipped the end of a cabbage into my basket. Plus three eggs that she insisted was my ration. I think that she was giving me her share and I protested very loudly. But she insisted that I take them and told me not to be so foolish.

I hugged her and told her how much I miss her. She is my true friend and I am lucky to have her, even if her breath grows worse by the day.

Wednesday, 28th April

The nights are getting cooler. At dusk the cicadas no longer make such a racket. Thankfully, we have fewer mosquitoes. Instead ticks plague us. Yesterday I had to cut one out of my leg. The wound bled and bled. Now both Emily and I wear bandages. Also my new Master tells me to watch out for the leeches that breed by the river. He tells me that he uses these creatures to drain blood from sick people. But he also says that leeches are not good for healthy people, and must be burnt off with a candle.

Last night Winston was granted an unexpected

night's leave. After supper, the four of us sat before the fire. I sat closest for I needed the light for patching and darning. This family's linen is so neglected, I am grateful to Mama for having shown me how to sew.

Surgeon Russell is kind, if a little absentminded. I like to pretend that he is my new papa, and that I am Winston and Emily's sister. Though Winston shows his wariness towards a convict girl, the Surgeon treats me almost like one of his family. But no matter how gentle he is, sooner or later someone will say something to remind me that I have fewer rights than a chicken or a cow.

My Master has received a letter from a Lieutenant Maxwell stationed on South Head. He told us that Maxwell writes that those at the Lookout are able to grow vegetables and catch a few fish. But the folk left in Sydney Cove are dangerously short of food, and he wonders what will become of them.

As he spoke, Winston looked more and more upset. When he could longer contain himself he cried, "Too much misery and selfishness! Folk are even mean about lending their cooking pots. I heard of an elderly convict who died while waiting for a kettle to cook his food. When they opened him up, they saw his stomach was empty."

"Things will improve very shortly," his father said sharply. "The council appointed by Governor Phillip has ordered the storeship *Supply* to sail to Batavia."

"How much food can a 170-ton ship carry? She is far too small."

"You are right," said his father. "But the captain has been told to hire another storeship. However it is a six month voyage. In that time we must pray for a miracle."

"Miracles!" Winston cried contemptuously. "Miracles only happen in the Bible and I wonder if even they can be true."

My eyes widened in alarm. Though I also wonder about the Bible, I would never confess this aloud. Sure as day turns into night, I would be punished. I waited for Winston's papa to give him a scolding. Instead the Surgeon merely smiled and puffed a little harder on his pipe.

A little later Winston asked his papa what else Lieutenant Maxwell reported.

The Surgeon emptied his pipe into the hearth. "Why, that he scans the horizon at sunrise and sunset in the hope of glimpsing a sail. He writes that sometimes he has been deceived by low-lying cloud into thinking it might be a vessel."

"What will happen if they do not come soon?"

My Master stretched long legs towards the fire. "Many folk may not survive. It is hard to collect food when we have so little shot and only two fishing boats."

Winston sprang to his feet to prowl around the hut. "What if the Second Fleet never arrives? What if the ships have foundered in a storm like the *Sirius*? Or they have lost their way?"

At this, such a gloom spread over us, I was almost sorry that I am still alive. Surely it would be easier and quicker to drown at sea than to slowly die of starvation.

But Winston's moods are so changeable. Suddenly he had had enough of all our misery and he turned to me to cry, "Come now Lizzie." He threw another stick into the hearth. "You must tell us how you came to be transported."

While he waited for my answer, a wind blew up outside. A branch tapped against the other side of the wall. We shivered and drew closer to the hearth. This southern land is so dark and forbidding. Though no one says this aloud, we secretly wonder what monsters and cannibals can be out there. What if they are merely biding their time to attack?

Winston repeated his request. I replied that my life

story was not so interesting. But the Surgeon insisted that I should stop being bashful.

So I put down my sewing and began. Edward, we shared our early years, so I will not bother to write down all I told them. But now they know how Papa had leased his land from Sir George Grainger. How Mama had been dressmaker to his wife, Lady Jane, and how that good lady had sent me to Doctor Nelson to learn my letters. Only when I came to the time our parents were sick from the Influenza and then died, did my voice falter.

Emily was awake and drinking in every word. "Poor you," she cried. "I know what that is like. My mama went to Heaven too."

We hugged and consoled each other. The Surgeon patted my shoulder when I started to cry. Only Winston seemed unmoved. He wanted to know what had happened to me then.

I told him how you, Edward, were only six, and too young to send away. And how my mama's younger sister Flossie took you in as one of her own. But I was already nine, old enough to start work. Because Mama had shown me how to sew, it was decided to apprentice me to a milliner in London. That was when my troubles began.

I would have told them more, only my Master said that it was very late, and that I should finish my story another time.

We laid our pallets on the floor and settled onto them. But so many memories kept running through my head, it took me ages to fall asleep.

Thursday, 29th April

Once more to the river to gather wild spinach. On our way an animal the size of a roasting pig with a pointy snout and spines like a porcupine waddled across our path. Emily wanted to know its name. I had to confess that I had never seen one before.

When we came to our favourite bend by the river, we found enough spinach to fill my basket. Then we settled onto our log to dangle our feet in the water. I was hoping that the native girl might return. Sure enough, I heard a light crackle behind me and there she was.

This time she approached us more openly. She carried her sleeping baby on her back in a woven basket. Holding out some roasted meat, she showed that it was safe by chewing a piece herself. From another grass basket, this one around her waist, she took out another morsel. I found it delicious – something between chicken and fish. I urged Emily to try some as I thought it could do us no harm. Emily did, and though at first she found the flavour strange, we were so hungry, the meat disappeared very quickly.

All this time, the girl was smiling and watching our every move. Though her skin was covered in oil and smelt like stale fish, I had never seen anyone with such splendid dark eyes or even white teeth.

When all the meat had gone, she searched in her basket and handed us two small cakes. They tasted something like bread, but very coarse. Because some of my teeth are broken and decayed, I had to chew very carefully. Finally, she offered us two sticks covered in honey and showed us how to suck on them. They were delicious. The best thing we have eaten in a very long time.

Now the baby gave a little cry. She removed him from his basket and he blinked and smiled as if he knew we wanted to play. Emily held out her arms. His mother handed him over, and I helped Emily hold him while we tickled his hands and toes and made him laugh.

Certainly he was the happiest baby I have seen since leaving Cranham.

Suddenly an older man, also an Indian, stepped out of the bushes. He carried several spears and what I think must be other weapons. His beard and hair were thick with dust and grime, his skin covered in oil and he also smelt most foul.

I handed the baby back to his mother and flung my arms around Emily. What if this man ate children? I knew that Indians had speared several convicts. Some had even died from their wounds.

But the savage took as little notice of us as had the porcupine-pig. Instead he spoke sternly to the girl. She hung her head. It was clear that he was chastising her for being with us. I felt very sorry for her.

They all disappeared into the bush as silently as they had come.

Then my heart nearly jumped into my mouth.

A man! This one white and hiding in the bushes behind us. How long had he been there? Then I realized that it was only Simple Sam. The poor man is so lonely he must be looking for friends. If I had been alone, I might have paused to chat with him awhile. Instead I yelled, "Off with you Sam," and he crashed through some bushes and disappeared.

After all this excitement, Emily was very tired. Though she protested that she wanted to walk, I piggybacked her home and made her rest on her pallet until sunset.

Friday, 30th April

Spent all day catching up on household tasks and teaching Emily to write her first words. EMILY, she wrote in the dust. Then CAT and DOG.

I told her how pleased I was with her and added that soon she will read and write as well as her papa.

But even this small activity tires her. Though I force her to eat wild spinach in the hope that this will bring more colour into her cheeks, too often her breathing turns shallow and raspy. Purple shadows circle her eyes, and her cheeks seem pale as death.

Winston did not appear for supper. My Master tells me that he must spend most nights in the barracks. The militia oversees those convicts working in the fields to ensure none run away to China. But there is a twinkle in my Master's eye as he tells me this.

Perchance he is not serious.

Where exactly IS China? I am sure that we would not have been quite as hungry if our fleet had landed there instead of Botany Bay. My Master has instructed me to make soup out of wild spinach, salted pork bones and rice. He said, "It would probably not hurt to throw in some hard tack. Our aching teeth will enjoy the softness."

I did as he suggested. After we settled at the table, he prayed, "For what we are about to receive, may the Lord make us truly thankful..."

We ate the soup very quickly. And loudly wished that there was more.

Sunday, 2nd May

Emily's lessons go well. She can now read many words starting with the letter B: BAR, BIRD, BONE, BELL, BOLT.

As a reward, and this being Sunday, I took her to visit Sarah.

Sarah was pleased to see us, though very busy. She

has another girl to help her look after Master Dodd. The girl's name is Jane, and I thought her a plain Jane indeed as she could barely smile us a greeting. Sarah says that she performs well enough. It seems that Jane has not enough sense to question directions, but that she has enough to follow them.

"What do you hear from Sydney Cove?" I asked as soon as we arrived. Because Master Dodd was, and still is, close to Governor Phillip, they get the latest news very quickly.

Sarah has only contempt for the militia. However, in her eyes Governor Phillip can do little wrong. She likes to remind me that it is a rare governor who insists that everyone, both freeman and convict, share equal rations when there is not enough food to go around.

"Little to report, though Lieutenant Ross is no longer with us," she replied. "The Master reports that Governor Phillip says he was a most disagreeable deputy. Always whining and bad tempered so it's a good thing that he's gone to Norfolk Island where he can do less harm than here. Only I pity those poor souls that have gone with him."

Outside the window, two greyish-brown birds with large beaks were setting up such a cackle she had to wait for them to stop. "And one more thing," she added. "The Governor thinks he must cut our rations further."

"Surely not," I cried. "How will we survive?" Not even Sarah handing me four pullet eggs – one for each of us – could make me smile. I was very careful to thank her. I am not sure if Sarah should be giving them to us. If she is found out she may be severely punished. At Rose Hill we are not restricted to such harsh rationing as those in Sydney Cove. But there is still hardly enough to fill our bellies.

Again I have been dreaming about the rich milk and cream our mama's cow, Daisy, used to produce. Also I like to imagine that I am eating slices of oven fresh bread smothered in butter and gooseberry jam. Rich meat pies with lashings of mashed potato and gravy. New season peas, beans and apples. Wild strawberries and berries plucked from the hedgerows.

My poor belly. How it cries out for more food.

Tuesday, 4th May

This morning Emily asked me why I would not play with her.

I was sweeping the hut with my brushwood broom. "As you see," I said impatiently, "I have too much else to do."

"Cannot the animals do this for you?"

I paused in my sweeping. "Maybe they could. Back home, some housewives would clean a chimney by throwing a fowl into it."

Her eyes grew large. "Did not the fowl protest?"

I giggled. "Surely it did. It would stalk out of the house most indignantly, even though it was covered in soot."

But Emily is right. I am much too busy, though not half as busy as if I was home. This is because I have no dough to set, no milk to churn, no poultry to chase away from under chairs and tables, no fruit and vegetables to preserve. Instead I use a branch to swat insects away and wonder where our next meal will be coming from.

Wednesday, 5th May

Last night Winston turned up saying he had two days leave and would spend them with his family. We sat around the fire, the Surgeon smoking his pipe, Emily resting on her pallet.

Soon as the sun fell into the horizon, Winston asked for more of my story.

"Indeed, Lizzie, you must," said my Master. "It does my children much good to hear how others manage their misfortunes."

Winston is so prickly he took immediate offence. "Papa, you think I do not know?"

My Master merely smiled and shook his head. He took a stick from the fire to light his pipe and puffed on it.

One of his stockings – the toe is vanished completely – must be patched. First I settled myself to my sewing. Then I began by telling them how I had left all Mama and Papa's possessions with Aunt Flossie who was to be your new mama…

∿∿∿∿∿∿

Edward, should this journal reach you, please make sure that our aunt returns Mama's four chairs, two bedsx and our table. Also, many of the kitchen pots, pans, mugs and plates belong to us, as does our plough-horse's almost new bridle. Do not forget to take the two milking buckets, Papa's spades, hatchet, wheelbarrow, cart and grindstone, and Mama's spinning wheel.

Edward, I do not know what has happened to our parents' house. Nor the land that Papa ploughed. Before I left for London I made our uncle promise not to let anyone else move in. But four years later, perhaps he has forgotten. Like our papa and his papa before him, you are now that farm's tenant and the land is yours to work.

I told the Russells how I had journeyed to London with my few clothes, six shillings in my pocket and a small packet of bread and meat. It took the chaise nearly a week to arrive. Then the streets seemed filled with so many drunken folk and beggars, I was fearful to dismount and very sorry I had ever left home.

My new Mistress had sent a man to bring me to her house. He led me through a warren of lanes and alleyways, all made dark and filthy with soot and animal droppings. There was so much noise from carriages rolling past and street peddlers, I was sure that if I stayed, I would very shortly become deaf.

Winston's cough was disbelieving. "Truly that bad?"

"Truly that bad," I said indignantly. How can Winston question me when I know that he has never been to London? "Even at night the streets wear a pall of smoke from too many coal fires. Only the main streets are lit by oil lamps. The streets have so much refuse and so many open sewers, a person could die from the stench. I had to hold my nose so I could manage to arrive at my new Mistress's house without vomiting."

I paused for breath. In the silence I noticed that the wind had dropped. I said, "Did I tell you that I was apprenticed to a milliner?"

Winston cleared his throat. "That you did."

I glanced around the room. Emily had fallen asleep. How much of my story had she heard? The Surgeon puffed his pipe and sat behind a fug of smoke. The fire cast strange shadows. Outside the window, the southern sky was ablaze with stars.

"Mistress Mary Clarke," I went on, "hated to spend a penny if ever a farthing would do. She used her apprentices as domestics as well as seamstresses. I slept on a narrow mattress in the attic. This bed I shared with Nancy Parke, the other apprentice."

"Two girls and one bed?" said my Master.

"From what I saw in London, I was lucky to have even that," I replied.

He puffed on his pipe and motioned for me to continue.

"We rose at dawn, worked hard all day and did not see our bed until late at night. For this we were given a little bread and sometimes a mutton chop."

"What must you do in exchange?" Winston asked.

I glanced up from my sewing. His gaze was fixed on the fire. Right now Mistress Clark's house felt like a very bad dream from which I had thankfully woken.

I explained how I had to empty the slops into the street and the fireplaces of ashes. I fetched water, laundered clothes, dusted, swept, and helped the cook prepare my Mistress's dinner. Between those tasks, I learned how to cut, shape, sew and iron various fabrics. Then I would carry the finished bonnet to whoever had ordered it. This way I saw much of the city.

Winston said, "What d–did you think of London town?"

I paused to think. "A bigger place of contrasts would be hard to find. Gentlefolk wear coats and dresses made of fine silk and satins. Their powdered wigs are so high they make the wearer seem twice as tall. Once they are clad in their best, they walk London's great streets and squares and meet in the pleasure gardens of Ranelagh and Vauxhall."

"So much for the rich," he said. "And the poor?"

"Why they live in a wilderness where there is always the threat of death from gangs of ruffians and general lawlessness. The poor only stop themselves from cutting their own throats by drinking too much gin."

"Surely the runners keep this in check?"

I shook my head. "The runners are only permitted to carry lanterns and wooden batons. They are poorly paid. To survive they must take bribes. Thieving is so common, it is whispered that the King himself was robbed while walking in his gardens in Kensington."

"That has long been coffee-house gossip," the Surgeon butted in, "and hardly worth repeating." A log slipped out of the fire. He carefully replaced it. Then he said, "Tell us more about your work."

I looked up from my stitching and said, "I was quick to learn and my Mistress was pleased with me. As time went on, she found more and more for me to do."

Winston said, "Why did not the other apprentice take her share?"

I picked up another stocking, and leaned towards the fire for more light to thread my needle. "Her sewing was not as skillful. And she was lazy. From certain looks she sent me, I soon learned that it was not beyond her to hate her fellow servants. And it did not take long before her hatred took solid form."

At this my Master roused himself with a start. He patted my shoulder somewhat awkwardly, then decided that it must be bedtime. "Lizzie, you will tell us more tomorrow."

Winston helped me lay the pallets on the floor and we settled down to sleep. Soon my Master's snores rang through the hut. But I was so tired nothing short of a tempest at sea could have kept me awake.

Thursday, 6th May

This morning I laundered Emily's linen in lye and hot water. Her clothes are so worn, I fear that with another washing they will shred too far to patch.

While I worked, I let my mind wander over all that has happened to me. Relating my story brings up so many memories. Many are so horrid, I wish I could forget them. But when Emily asked me what my parents looked like, I found that I could hardly remember. Lately Mama's face has become confused with Sarah's. And Papa begins to look like Henry Dodd and sometimes Surgeon Russell.

Edward, how different if we had been rich. Wealthy folk hire artists to paint them so they cannot forget what their loved ones look like. I remember our mama telling me that when Lady Grainger was young she was so beautiful, artists clamoured to paint her portrait. The Surgeon wears a locket on his heart. Inside the locket is a miniature of Mary Russell, his dead wife. When he showed it to me, I examined her very carefully. Her hair was yellow, and she had blue eyes, pink cheeks and a mole on her left cheek. Her children look like her in that both are fair-skinned and delicately built.

My eyes are sore, and I am very tired. Enough writing for tonight.

Sunday, 9th May

This morning Master Henry Dodd called everyone to join him under a stand of red gums. He began the service with "The Lord's Prayer" and then "Rock of Ages". The militia's drummer and fife accompanied our singing. But many felt too low to join in.

Halfway through "Rock of Ages" the skies opened up. Soon our clothes were drenched. Leaves and twigs squelched under our feet. Streams trickled into puddles.

Master Dodd ignored the rain and stood on a log to deliver his sermon. He is a plain man with a round face, pockmarked skin hidden under coarse brown hair and a three day beard. His blunt speech and manner remind me of our papa's. He urged us to keep up our spirits, saying that if we neglected to pray, all would be lost. He promised us that any day more ships would sail from Cape Town into Sydney Cove. These ships will carry enough provisions to last us until more crops could be reaped.

"What if the ships don't come?" someone called from the crowd.

"What if Noah had not prayed?" he answered right back. "Remember how Noah and his family stayed on their ark 40 days and 40 nights? Why, if Noah had lost faith, none of us would be here."

Not everyone could accept this. Someone called, "Perchance Noah had enough to fill his belly, and faith to him were easier."

Another cried, "Noah had all those animals to eat if he were hungry."

"Yes, yes. We're starving too much to pray."

If they thought this could silence Master Dodd, they were sorely mistaken. He reminded us of how brave we had been at sea. How in the coldest and stormiest leg of our journey we had helped each other survive. He finished off by describing all our achievements this last year in Rose Hill, telling us how we were so much better off than anyone in Port Jackson.

This year there has been little rain and by the time his sermon was over, the sky was a rich deep blue. A flock of scarlet, green and yellow Rose Hillers flew overhead. Someone shouted that this was a good omen, and we set off for our huts far more cheerfully than we had left them.

After our sparse dinners, my Master said that he

would stay with Emily and he gave me a few hours to spend however I might desire. I went to visit Sarah. Over a cup of liquorice tea, she told me that there is talk in Sydney Cove that everyone, and this includes the militia and even their officers, must take turns catching fish. Picturing some of those proud men casting lines and then having to scale and gut those smelly creatures, made us laugh most heartily.

"Not that Winston will mind too much," I said. "I think he enjoys fishing."

She said, "Have you two become friends?"

"Winston is never rude. But he always lets me know that he is militia and I am a convict. Besides..." I frowned uncertainly, "perchance I imagine it, but whenever he addresses me, his stammer grows worse."

She smiled knowingly. "That young man must learn how often it's only luck that separates rich from poor."

I hugged her. Maybe Sarah cannot read and write or say her words properly, but she is truly a wise woman. She hugged me back, crying, "I really miss you, Lizzie. Jane does her job well enough, but she ain't no fun to be with."

"I miss you too, Sarah," I cried and we held each other a very long time.

When I got back to the Russell's, Emily was lying

on her pallet, sobbing as if her little heart would break. "Where were you, Lizzie?" she cried. "I thought you were gone forever."

I placed her on my lap, saying, "I was only visiting Sarah. You and me are great friends and you know that I will never part from you."

"But my mama said that," she sobbed, "and then she went to Heaven…" She buried her head in my chest.

She was so hot and feverish it took me an hour to calm her down. Fortunately Sarah had found enough flour to bake Emily a heart-shaped biscuit. I showed it to her and she brightened up very quickly.

Monday, 10th May

A morning of misfortune. Emily is still feverish and refuses to eat. Her father tells me that I must force her to drink as much water as possible. But even water makes her throw up. I have seen this illness before. It comes from our salt meat, which is so rotten my Master thinks that we would be healthier only eating dried peas, oats and rice and whatever vegetables that can be passed our way.

To add to my distress, while laundering I dropped a full cauldron of boiling water. I narrowly missed scalding my feet. Then I had to fetch more water and find more wood to fill the wood-box. To add to my annoyance, our last sliver of soap slid into the cauldron and melted away completely. To make more soap, I need potash and animal fat. Of course I have none. I worry that if the Surgeon hears about these misadventures, he might want another servant. Someone stronger and less clumsy.

By late afternoon, I had brought all the washing inside. It looked clean enough, though with more rips for me to mend. Emily was no longer as feverish and I had her drinking a little water and nibbling on a biscuit.

Pease porridge and rice for supper. The Surgeon did not arrive until well after sunset. He looked so weary, with barely enough energy to light his pipe, that I felt very sorry for him. He tells me that shortly we must all move back to Sydney Cove for he is needed there to help the sick. I pray that this will not happen too soon.

"Of course, Lizzie, you will come with us," he said. But as that means I must leave Sarah behind, I am in two minds over this, even though I would dearly like to see what is happening in Sydney Cove.

This morning Emily had a little more colour in her cheeks. I am sure that it is the wild herbs I force her to eat though she always groans and complains that they are far too bitter.

She finished her lessons and demanded a reward. I clapped my hands and sang her a rhyme Mama sang to you, Edward:

Intery, mintery, cuttery corn,
Brambly briar and brambly thorn,
Wire, briar, barrel, lock,
Three geese in a flock.
One flew east and one flew west,
And one flew over the cuckoo's nest.

When we got to the end, I tickled Emily's ribs like Mama did ours. Emily laughed so much I sang and sang until I could not manage another croak. Edward, I think that in some ways Emily has replaced you in my mind. Not that I love you any the less. You are still my closest living relative. But you are so far away, who knows if we shall ever see each other again? All I can hope is that this journal will sooner or later arrive in Cranham. And then you will know that I have never forgotten you.

Winston arrived shortly before supper carrying four pink and grey cockatoos. We are hungry enough to eat anything that walks, crawls or flies, but it pained me to see those pretty birds so dead and bedraggled. Winston started to tell me how he had trapped them and wrung their necks. I shuddered and told him that I had rather not know.

"It won't stop you eating them, will it?" he snapped at me impatiently.

We would have quarrelled then and there, only he picked up the birds and stalked off. When he returned, I saw that he had cut off their heads and gutted them.

I dipped the carcasses in boiling water, plucked their feathers and skewered them on sticks. Now I could pretend that they were only chickens. But I was still very cross. I told myself that Winston might think he is all grown because he is a member of the Royal

Marines. But he is just a teasing boy. If I once thought we might be friends, then I was sorely mistaken.

When his papa arrived home we cooked the birds over the fire and ate them with a little pease pudding. The taste reminded us of wild fowl, though it was a little more gamy.

Supper over, Emily reminded her papa that she wished to hear more of my story.

The Surgeon lit his pipe and drew on it. "We have quite a Scheherazade in Lizzie," he told his children. "Perchance there are things she might not want to relate."

"Not true, sir," I cried hotly. "God knows I have nothing to hide."

"Except for a bad temper," Winston murmured.

I was about to answer that I am only bad tempered when sorely provoked. Just in time I bit my tongue. Edward, our mama always said that I let it run away with me. I must remind myself that I am only a servant, a girl and a convict. They can dismiss me whenever they please. But it is hard to stay silent when others are being stupid or insensitive. Thankfully Emily cried, "Who is Scheherazade?"

The Surgeon reached out to stroke his daughter's arm. "Why, she was a beautiful lady who must tell a thousand and one stories so as not to lose her head."

Emily giggled and slid her thumb into her mouth. She does not always take her papa and brother as seriously as I must.

The Surgeon turned to me, "On with your story, Scheherazade," he said mock sternly, "or we will be too sleepy to listen."

I had almost forgotten where I had left off, but Winston quickly reminded me.

I took my sewing closer to the fire. Then I started on how Nance, the other apprentice, had been fifteen and grown. And how I could not help noticing that she and Silas, who was our manservant, spent much time whispering in corners when they thought no one saw them. My Mistress had already told us how several small things had gone missing: a gold ribbon, two bobbins of thread, and a small pair of scissors. When she discovered that a silken gown and matching bonnet – these made for a fine lady – were also missing, she set up such a cry, one might have thought everything she owned had been stolen.

She brought Silas, Nance and myself into her workroom to question us. We insisted that we knew nothing about it. My Mistress fixed us with a glare that could kill a grown man. "Goods worth over seven shillings," she cried. "If any of you have taken them, why I will have you in gaol before you can count to ten."

She combed through the attic where Nance and I slept. I had tied the six shillings I had brought with me into a kerchief and hidden this in my wooden box. I had hoped that while I was in London I might earn a guinea or two. Then my plan was to return to Cranham and use the money to keep Edward and myself in modest comfort.

Immediately my Mistress found this money, she decided that it was hers, and that I had stolen it. No matter how much I protested my innocence, she called the runners, and they marched me off to gaol.

Here Winston cut in. "Did you not say the money was yours?"

Tears rolled down my cheeks. "I did. But I was nine years old and an apprentice. Who would believe me?"

"D–Did you know who had really stolen those clothes?"

"I am sure that Silas and Nance plotted it together. They must have stolen those other things too. Shortly after I went to prison they left my Mistress' house to open a tavern. Where else would they have found the money to do that?"

What I did not say was how in the beginning I could hardly believe that this was really happening, that it was not all a terrible dream from which I would shortly wake. I found myself behind bolted doors. The turnkeys punished me most severely for having no money. But I had lost everything that was most precious to me and I had done nothing wrong. Nothing.

"Tell my children more about the gaol," said the Surgeon. "These are places to inspire dread even in the most hardened criminal."

I shuddered and went on to say that whatever they had heard about those places cannot equal their true horror. I was thrown into a cell with the most evil criminals. My few things were quickly stolen, and I think I was lucky not to be strangled or stabbed.

The law stated that I must be tried by a judge before three days were up. It was December and the middle of winter. Those on trial had to wait their turn in an open courtyard. This yard was so cold the puddles froze under our feet. An icy wind cut through the few rags we wore. When they brought me into Justice Hall, the first thing I saw was how both judge and jury carried nosegays of fresh herbs. These were to protect them from the stench coming from us prisoners.

Here my Master broke in to explain how the herbs

were also used as a protection against prison fever or typhus, a most deadly disease. He turned to me to say, "You were fortunate not to catch it."

Winston yawned as if weary. But I knew he wanted to hear more, because he stammered, "W–Was anyone allowed into the Court to watch your case?"

I laughed wryly. "Why, it was better than a Punch and Judy show. The court was filled with people who made fun of everything. They called out, making judgements that had nothing to do with the guilt or innocence of the accused."

"What did the judge want to know?"

"My name, and how old I was, and my occupation. And then if I was guilty of this crime. I answered him as truthfully as I knew how. Then he called my Mistress onto the stand. She gave them such a pack of lies. She said that I had always been lazy and that I could never be trusted. Of course the judge only listened to her. My fate was sealed in less than fifteen minutes."

"Did you not protest?"

"I did, but it did me no good whatsoever…"

My Master openly shuddered. The fire was burning low. He heaped more wood onto it, then turned to say, "Tomorrow I have much to do. Lizzie, you must continue your story another time."

I rose from my stool and he helped me arrange our pallets on the floor. The nights are growing cold. I wished I had a warm quilt to lay over Emily. Her papa guessed my thoughts and covered her with his coat. She stirred but did not wake. She needs a lot of sleep. I notice that the Surgeon's coat is torn in three places. But I have no dark thread with which to fix it. Perchance Sarah will have some.

There is just enough fire-light to finish this off.

Wednesday, 12th May

All morning, Emily pleaded with me to patch Mary, her cloth doll. The poor thing has lost an arm and a leg and every seam has split. I promised her that I would. Then added, "But first you must practise your letters."

In the dust outside our hut, we wrote "The Lord is my shepherd."

Once she had printed this, I tried a rhyme my old teacher, Doctor Nelson, had shown me:

Knock on the door,

Peep in,
Lift up the latch,
Walk in.

Emily copied this almost perfectly, though she still gets her D's mixed up with her B's and wrote "boor" instead of "door".

I had intended to spend the rest of the morning dusting and sweeping, but Emily pleaded with me to take her to Sarah's. Seems that Sarah has promised Emily a sweet biscuit. I cannot imagine that a single grain of sugar is to be found anywhere in Rose Hill.

After her lessons, Emily was so tired, I piggybacked her most of the way to Master Dodd's hut. Though she is small for her age and her arms and legs are like sticks, lately my shoulders hurt whenever I carry her.

I am always fearful when walking this track. Just when we had passed the convict huts, she let out a scream.

My heart leapt into my mouth.

Emily pointed towards a clump of straggly gum trees. Someone was hiding behind them.

When I saw who it was, I sighed in relief. "Simple Sam will not harm you," I assured her. "He only wants to play with us."

Sam emerged from the bushes, his face so dirty and covered in scabs, his own mother would not recognize him. Poor Sam cannot control his limbs, and he twitches and dribbles like a baby. Since he approached Emily that day by the river, my Master thinks that he is dangerous. He tells me that he intends asking Master Dodd to send Sam back to Sydney Cove. But I feel sorry for Sam, and I pray that my Master will change his mind.

Sam's handicaps never stop him from trying to tell me things. Not that anything he says makes sense. We listened for a few moments. But as Emily was growing more and more anxious, clutching my neck and whimpering, I quickly waved goodbye and left.

Sarah was pleased to see us, though very busy. They are hoping for a visit from Governor Phillip. Master Dodd insists that the hut be made more comfortable. It seems that when the Governor came last February, he complained that he was sick, and that sleeping on a straw pallet on the floor was not to his liking.

I said, "Did he not praise us for all we have achieved in Rose Hill?"

Sarah shook her head. "Indeed he seemed sorely disappointed. He were saying that even if this farm had more than a hundred convicts, that we can never grow enough to feed the entire colony. I can remember his exact words. 'Experience sirs'," she said in as perfect English as I have ever heard, "'has taught me how difficult it is to make men industrious who have passed their lives in habits of vice and indolence'."

Emily giggled and pleaded for more. Sarah can mimic anyone. Back in London, before she went to gaol, she worked in a playhouse, and she can make herself sound like anything she chooses. So she barked like a dog, meowed like a cat and quacked like a duck.

Emily laughed and laughed. I am sure that so much laughing can only do her good, even though her papa urges me to keep her as quiet as possible.

"Lizzie, I hear good reports of your new Master, Surgeon Russell," Sarah told me. "The men say he can cure their sicknesses with leeches. And he also tells them to avoid the salt meat, and to eat wild spinach and trap animals."

"Do they listen to him?"

"I think some must. Certainly they are healthier."

Before we left, she gave me two duck eggs, and told me to cook them in a pan together with some ship's biscuit and potato tops, as this would make a tasty flan. But Emily was disappointed, as Sarah had to confess that there is not a single grain of sugar left in all of Rose Hill. Not even in exchange for rum.

Tonight we ate the flan with a good appetite. After I cleaned our tin plates, we settled in front of the fire. Keeping my promise, I started patching Mary, Emily's doll. "Why do you call your doll Mary?" her papa asked.

The child's lower lip trembled. "Papa, you know Mama's name was Mary. It stops me missing her so much."

I glanced at Winston He also looked ready to weep. He pretends to be strong and to enjoy teasing girls. But I think that he refuses to show his true feelings as he thinks this is unmanly.

Before everyone sank into a permanent gloom, the Surgeon turned to me. "Come now, Scheherazade, let Emily and Winston hear more of your story."

I shook my head. "Sir, Scheherazade invented her stories. Mine are quite true…"

"Yes, yes." He patted my shoulder. "Once your life was most perilous and it is surely a miracle that you are still alive. But now you are safe with us and little can befall you. So you must tell us about your stay in Newgate Prison."

I sighed a little. Then I settled closer to the fire and began.

Briefly, I told them how some poor folk claim going to gaol is little different from being cast onto the streets of London. Certainly the cells had no furniture, and every corner was knee-deep in filth. Nor did the turnkeys provide us with straw or clothes, and there was hardly anything to eat. Rich prisoners bought what they needed from the turnkeys who made great fortunes out of other people's misery. The poor could only steal from each other. Many died of starvation and disease.

My Master said, "How did you manage?"

"Sir," I said. "I would certainly be dead if Sarah had not found me."

A log slipped out of the fire. My Master carefully replaced it. A possum ran over the roof making a hissing sound. The noise reminded me of the women I had met in Newgate who quarrelled and stole each other's few belongings.

When I was pushed into my cell, I was so frightened I just wanted to die. Sarah found me crouched against a wall, my eyes tightly shut. A gaggle of women was trying to steal the few things I had managed to bring with me.

My Master said, "Did she not approach you as yet another thief?"

I said that I thought she had, and that was why she chased the other women away. But then we had started to talk and I told her all that had befallen me. She must have had much need of a friend, because very quickly she told me much about herself. She was a married woman. But her husband had treated her so harshly she had had to knife him to protect herself. Though her husband was not badly hurt, he called for the runners and had his wife sent to gaol.

I paused to examine my stitching. My Master took the opportunity to lean forward to take a lighted twig from the fire and light his pipe. "I am almost out of tobacco," he said regretfully. "A small loss. But my pipe is such a comfort." He turned to me, "Come now, Scheherazade, continue."

I looked up from my sewing. "Sarah said to me, 'I have little in the world to live for. And neither have you. So we will protect each other'."

"And Scheherazade, did she?"

"Sir, she most certainly did. Without her protection I would not be here."

In the pause that followed, my Master knocked his pipe against the hearth to empty it. I note that he mostly calls me Scheherazade. But when he forgets and calls me Lizzie, he lingers over my name – almost as if it has some special meaning for him. I think that once he was attached to another "Lizzie". I would like to ask him who this was, but I think he would see this as far too bold for a convict-servant.

He turned to his son to say sternly, "Learn from this story how a single misfortune can ruin a man's future."

Winston yawned and ignored his papa's message.

"Enough for tonight," the Surgeon murmured. "I am tired and Emily is already asleep."

We checked that no logs could fall out of the hearth and settled our pallets on the floor. I can just manage to stay awake long enough to write this down.

Thursday, 13th May

My Master came home to tell us that we will be leaving for Sydney Cove in two days' time. He said a message had come from the Governor. It seems that every surgeon in the colony is needed there.

I was so excited. I have been in Rose Hill for nearly a year. All this time I have longed for news from

England. Not that any ships have called into Port Jackson, but it is hard to wait for a messenger who must come all the way from Sydney. Also, I was interested to see how the settlement had changed, or if it had at all.

Emily's lessons over, I piggybacked her to Sarah's to deliver my news.

Sarah immediately broke into loud sobs. I flung my arms around her saying, "Please don't cry. I am not going forever."

"But you're almost grown," she wept. "What if you meet a fancy man and marry him?"

I giggled. "Not likely."

She grunted and quickly went on to talk of other things. "While you are in Sydney Cove, Lizzie, you must remember to be artful. On no account walk by yourself or just with the little one at night. And see that none of your few things are taken from you."

"I am always careful not to be robbed," I said indignantly.

"Be that as it may. With all our precautions, you may recall how easy it were last year for thieves to break into our bake-house and rob us blind."

I promised her that I would heed her advice. Then I assured her that I would be back in Rose Hill as soon as possible. All this time Emily had been playing outside the house drawing figures in the dust. She came inside and Sarah spent a long time cuddling her and making her promise to look after me. I think she is as fond of Emily as I am, and that she sometimes wishes that the little girl was hers.

Before we left, she kindly gave me four potatoes and four eggs and a leftover scrap of grey soap. She warned me to use the soap most sparingly. I wish that I had some of Mama's to give her. I remember Mama making soap and colouring the bars pink with beetroot and green with spinach. Sometimes Mama would add oatmeal to the mix to soften our skins.

Back home, I insisted Emily take a nap while I laundered everything we were taking to Sydney Cove. Then I boiled the potatoes and eggs Sarah had given me for our supper. The Surgeon came home well after sunset. He told me that Winston would be travelling to Sydney with us, but that he was to sleep in the barracks until then.

The Journey
Saturday, 15th May

Late last night my Master told me to pack everything we own. He says that there is hardly any food left in Sydney Cove and that we must prepare ourselves for the worst. I think that he is very sorry to be leaving Rose Hill.

Winston had hired a pony called Patch to carry Emily. A good horse and rider could manage the journey in less than a day. But when my Master caught sight of Patch, he shouted that Winston should have found us a better nag.

"You did not see the others," his son protested, and then he sulked and sulked until nightfall. Patch's ribs show through and she has a weeping sore on her right leg. But we have so few horses in Rose Hill, I think Winston was lucky to find her.

It is not my place to criticize my Master, but while he is very harsh with Winston, he is soft as dough with Emily. Perchance this is why Winston is wary of showing anyone his true feelings? Edward, I think that he misses his mama as much as I miss ours. Sometimes I hear him call for her in his sleep. Though when he wakes, he is always calm and distant.

This morning we left Rose Hill and Emily wheezed very badly. The men decided to piggyback her and use the pony to carry our packs. The track was so littered with boulders and fallen branches that we had to stop very often to help Patch through. My Master and Winston carried sticks in case we came across any escaped convicts or Indians. My Master reports that many Indians are sick with smallpox and influenza. So many are dying, he thinks that they have never had these maladies before.

Tonight we have camped by a stream. At dusk, a wicked wind blew up and we could not stop shivering. While the men went looking for firewood, I dressed Emily in all her shifts and petticoats to keep her warm, then wrapped her in my Master's coat so that only her face showed through.

Around us, huge gums with reddish bark rose into the sky. Their trunks were so wide a man's arms could barely encircle them. The wind shook their branches making their leaves tremble. Shivers ran down my spine. This land is awesomely strange.

What monsters were watching us from the shadows? What if they were just waiting to attack?

We supped on a little salt pork and hardtack, though there was hardly enough to touch the sides of our bellies. Then my Master turned to me. "Come now, Scheherazade," he cried – and I had to smile at my new name. "More of your story will help us forget how hungry we still are."

I was tired and would have liked to stay quiet. But my Master has shown me so much kindness I did not dare refuse. Drawing closer to the fire, I began, "Sir, what I did not know before I went to prison was that there were so many convicts, the government did not know where to send us…"

"That is true," my Master cut in as a wicked gust shook leaves and blew dust into our eyes. "But when Captain Cook returned from his great southern voyage, he praised the timber and flax he saw here." A log fell out of the fire. He leaned forward to push it back. "My apologies, Scheherazade. I interrupt your story, and my children will be angry. Pray continue."

So I told them how, for the first time in a year, we convicts were permitted to shuffle into the open and down to where Blackfriar's Bridge crosses the River Thames. I told them how wonderful it was to breathe fresh air and see people going about their everyday affairs.

When we reached the docks we were pushed onto barges that sailed to Portsmouth. There, we were imprisoned for many months in old ships called hulks where the spars and rigging had been removed. These hulks were dirty, dangerous places. Even worse than Newgate Prison.

"Yes, yes, we know all about that," Winston broke in impatiently. "Did you not tell us that Sarah Burke saved your life?"

"Indeed she did," I replied. "Many times."

Winston's eyes gleamed. I think he enjoys my stories, though he would never actually tell me this. He said, "Will you relate one to us?"

I thought back. "Perhaps the most dangerous time was when Rachel Bolton thought I was trying to steal her child…"

I thought my Master was half-asleep. Now he stirred himself enough to chuckle. "Steal a child? Why would she think that?"

I explained how I had only been trying to help a poor woman who was seriously ill. She had given birth to a boy in Newgate Prison, and her baby was choking on his own vomit. I had tried to clean his face so he

111

could breathe. But my action set the whole prison against me. The other women accused me of trying to kidnap the baby. When I protested that I had only been trying to save his life, no one believed me. Only Sarah protecting me with a sharp knife, saying she would use it on the first person that came too close, had kept me alive.

The hair on the back of my neck prickled as I recalled those crazy women crowding around, and how close to death I had been.

A loud sigh came from Emily. I turned to see if she was unwell, but she was sleeping most soundly. Winston asked, "What happened to the mother and child?"

"They died shortly after. So many maladies ran through the hulks, it was a miracle that any of us were strong enough to step on board the *Lady Penrhyn* and sail for Botany Bay…"

I would have continued, only my Master's hand stopped me. "Enough for tonight, Scheherazade," he said gravely. "More of this sorry tale will make us wakeful. Leave the rest for tomorrow."

While the others arranged themselves to sleep, I crept closer to the fire so I could still see enough to write in my journal. Though I am tired enough to sleep a whole week, there is too much keeping me awake: the wind swishing the upper branches, animals prowling through the undergrowth, shadows thrown by the fire, and my half-empty belly.

Winter is in the air. Yet strangely, I look on it with less dread than at home. Here, it never snows. Nor does it get too cold. But how strange to have Christmas in mid-summer and Easter heralding winter. I am sure that if I did not see this for myself, that I would think it a fiction, perhaps written by Mister Defoe.

Sunday, 16th May

Last night, an hour or so after falling asleep, I dreamed that I was back in Newgate Prison. Sarah was not there to protect me. That Turnkey, that same greedy fat man who crushed the toes on my left foot when I told him that I had no money, was using his clamp on my other foot. All I could do was scream and scream…

I woke with a start to find my foot in a bull-ants' nest. The wretched insects had bitten me and now my toes are red and itchy. Also, in the early hours of this morning Emily coughed and coughed. Then she threw up everything she had eaten the night before.

Her papa had brought with him some crushed tea-tree leaves. He instructed me to heat these leaves in a pan with some water. We put a shawl over Emily's head so she could inhale the fumes. Half an hour later, the worst of her gasping stopped. Even then the Surgeon decided that she was not well enough to travel, and that we should stay here another day.

Winston was most dreadfully disappointed. I think he can hardly wait to join the rest of his regiment. Secretly I was relieved. This morning I had woken with severe cramps in my belly. My Master says the salt-pork is rancid, and that it is responsible for all our troubles. Last night he looked me up and down with a critical eye and said, "A little more food, and perchance you would grow taller."

I did not know what to say. Whenever I complain to Sarah about being too small and thin, she will say "Lizzie, you might look a child, but after all your misfortunes, you do not think like one."

This morning the smoke from our fire brought

several visitors to our camp. The first was a man with piercing grey eyes, a most prominent nose with a bump in the middle, a balding head and a florid complexion.

Because he came in torn breeches, a sleeveless shirt and carried a musket, we thought he must be an escaped convict, and we sprang to our feet in fright.

My Master reached for his stick.

The man held out his hands to show us that he meant no harm. He bowed and quickly introduced himself as Lieutenant William Collins. He said, "My apologies for coming upon you like this. My uniform is so shabby, I only wear it when I am on duty."

Winston whispered to me that he knew this Lieutenant. It seems he was the first officer to step ashore at Botany Bay with a party of convicts to hoist the Union Jack.

(I think that sometimes Winston forgets that I am a girl, worse still a convict, and that he does not want us to be friends.)

The Lieutenant and my Master settled in front of the fire. We heard more of the situation in Sydney Cove. The Lieutenant reports that there is much stealing of food. The Governor has given each person or family a plot to grow vegetables. But the Lieutenant says that too many folk know little about farming, and even if they do, that they are too weak to work.

Winston repeated a rumour that many folk were dying from lack of vittles, and he wanted to know if this was true.

"There is food of a sort," Lieutenant Collins said reluctantly. "Some trap small animals. Others catch small fish. These squash the worst of our hunger. But such foods will not give our men strength. We need more salt beef, salt pork and salt mutton. Also, we are almost out of flour and rice..."

He stopped. We heard footsteps coming close.

My Master and Winston reached for their sticks.

The Lieutenant held up his musket.

A woman and a man were coming along the track. At first they seemed as startled to see us as we were to see them. Then they greeted us most amiably. The Lieutenant put his musket away. I am sure that he intended to use it only as a threat. There is hardly any ammunition left in all of Port Jackson.

These new people introduced themselves as Seaman Abel Flush and Mistress Margaret Stewart. Both were in their early twenties, and both were blue eyed and fair skinned, though considerably weathered. Margaret ties her curls into a leather string, just the way our mama wore hers whenever she had much to do.

They told us that they were heading for the Government Farm at Rose Hill. I could tell Margaret was a convict and probably not Abel's wife. She clung to his arm as if she was not sure if he would stay with her. Even so, she has a kind heart. When she saw how pale and weak little Emily was, she searched in her pack for a woollen shawl, insisting that Emily wear it to warm her chest.

My Master thanked her with tears in his eyes. All we could offer our visitors was liquorice tea. To everyone's delight, the Lieutenant produced a flask of rum from his pack. He poured a healthy tot into each mug. Though I dislike the taste, the rum's fiery warmth soothed my aching belly.

As we sat around the fire, somehow the conversation turned, as it often does, to home. Then to all the hardships we must suffer.

Lieutenant Collins said, "Sometimes when I am too hungry to sleep, I repeat the names of the ships in our fleet." He closed his eyes, "*Sirius. Alexander. Scarborough…*" He opened his eyes and laughed.

At this Margaret burst out, "Didn't this good Lieutenant sail on the *Sirius*?"

117

"I most certainly did," he replied. "And was most upset to learn that she has foundered on Norfolk Island. She was an excellent flagship."

Margaret stared at him impatiently. "So you can have no idea how it was for the rest of us." Her tone was bitter. "Those who sailed in the prison ships were packed in worse than animals. No portholes or windows. Any day the ships were in port *and* every night, each of us slept in an area not much bigger than a child's crib."

The Surgeon looked most disturbed. Though whether it was at Margaret's outburst, or what she was telling him, I could not say. He said that it was true that he did not see inside the prison ships, but surely it could not have been so bad as she described...

She would not let him finish. "We were like caged animals," she cried. "We could not stand up or move about without hurting ourselves. We had to lie perfectly still until the sun rose next morning."

"Nor were there any candles or lanterns to light our nights," I said, adding my own piece to her story.

Winston said, "Were not the captains frightened that these would set fire to their ships?"

"True enough," said Margaret. "And in bad weather the hatches were battened down. We lay in the dark lapped by heaving seawater, sewage and vomit. All we had as company were curses and groans…"

Before she could continue, Abel placed his hand over her mouth as if he feared that her angry outburst would get them into trouble. My Master glanced at the Lieutenant. A look passed between them. But whatever he was going to say, he must have decided against it, and there was a long silence as each of us recalled that eight and a half month voyage. Certainly for Sarah and myself, it had been much as Margaret described, though conditions were perhaps a little better on the *Lady Penrhyn* than on some of the other prison ships. Yet our lives were uncertain and only Sarah's courage saved me many times from being hurt.

Some of the women on the *Lady Penrhyn* were so miserable that all they did was quarrel. Occasionally our captain, William Cropton Sever, would get so angry at their foul language, he would order them to receive a severe lashing. When more sorely provoked, he had their hair cut off. Not that this did him much good as the women only cursed more loudly as they were being whipped and shaved.

Monday, 17th May

All night Emily coughed and wheezed most piteously. None of the Surgeon's inhalations could ease her distress. He said that she was still not well enough to travel and that we should rest here another day. Not that I mind, as I will use the time to fill my journal.

The Lieutenant had noticed me writing, and he wanted to know what ink I use. He says there is hardly any left in Sydney. I told him that my friend Sarah mixed certain barks, beet-skins and charcoal. Then she leaves this potion in a pot for two weeks to absorb the iron.

He picked up this book and glanced through some of the pages. "You have a fair hand. For a convict, that is," he finally commented. "Surgeon Russell tells me that you are teaching his little girl her letters."

"Sir, that I am," I replied.

His glance was shrewd. "You are not the only diarist in Port Jackson. Phillip keeps excellent records. Captain Watkin Tench also keeps a very full journal. Do you show your writings to others?"

I shook my head. Better not to mention that what I write, Edward, is for your eyes only. But ever since I had started this journal, something had been bothering me. "Sir," I said to the Lieutenant, "I intend posting this diary to my brother in England. But I do not know if the ink will last long enough for him to read my words."

He saw my point and poured a little rum into the ink to preserve it.

I thanked him very carefully. Then waited for him to turn to my Master before picking up my pen. Marines can take offence so easily. They are too easily provoked. Winston is like a prickly porcupine. If ever I speak to him, his answers are miserly – almost as if he cannot bear to spare me too many words. His lofty attitude always reminds me that I am a convict-girl and am thus to be despised. At the same time, he tells his papa that our legal system is unfair and that it should be changed.

"Why do you speak such rebellion?" my Master once asked him. "You question everything far too openly. In France there is much talk of revolution." He looked most concerned. "Winston, be careful or you will be sent to gaol for treason and trying to provoke a mutiny."

His son flushed angrily and his stammer grew worse. "H–How can we t–tolerate a system that allows so many hungry people to be hung and transported?"

It was on the tip of my tongue to remind Winston that his rebellion could start by being kinder to me, his convict-servant. But I thought better of it. Teasing him would only make things worse.

While we were thus gathered around the fire, my Master asked me to relate more of my story. At first I was too shy to speak in front of so many people and I shook my head. But when my Master insisted, I told them how Sarah and I were imprisoned for many months in the hulks. Here, conditions had been even grimmer than they had been in Newgate Prison. Many prisoners died from disease and neglect. Meanwhile Captain Phillip worked very hard at collecting the stores needed for such a long voyage. As my Master said, "Only a terrible outbreak of prison fever on the *Alexander* hurried things along. If we had brought everything on Captain Phillip's list, we would not presently be on such short rations."

Emily was awake and feeling slightly better. She joined in the conversation. "Why, Papa," she cried. "What did we leave behind?"

He reached over to stroke her cheek. "Clothing for

our women. Lime to make mortar to hold our bricks together, and we brought too few fishing nets. We certainly need more nails. Most importantly, there is no shot for our muskets so we cannot hunt for game."

The Lieutenant said, "At least Captain Phillip took enough food to last two years of settlement. He could hardly have known that our crops would fail."

My Master nodded grimly. "Although while we were on board ship, the food was not equally shared."

"True enough," Winston broke in. "The men c—convicts received only two thirds of the marines' rations. And the women only half."

The Lieutenants' eyebrows shot up. "You think the women deserved more?"

A faint noise made me glance around. Margaret was red faced with anger. She cried, "Many women were heavy with child or suckled small babies. They were feeding two mouths. They needed *more* food, not less. If those babies and children had been properly fed, many more might have lived."

She burst into loud sobs. Through her tears she managed to tell us that she had given birth while on board ship, but that her baby had died shortly after we left Cape Town.

This time Abel did not attempt to silence her. Even

123

the Lieutenant fell silent. I think he has a kinder heart than he would have had us believe. I placed my arms around Margaret and whispered, "This also happened to my friend Sarah. Her baby was stillborn."

Still tearful, Margaret managed a smile. "But I am once more with child." She patted her swollen belly. Though she hangs onto Abel's arm and looks into his eyes, deep inside I think that she has as much fire as Sarah and will suffer as little nonsense. Suddenly I heard a crackling noise. It came from behind me. I sprang to my feet, and shouted a warning. Someone was creeping up on us…

My Master has decided that Emily is well enough for us to continue our journey. He calls to me to quickly gather our belongings together.

Sydney Cove
Tuesday, 18th May

We are presently settled in our new home, and I have much to say about that. But first I must finish recording last Sunday's adventure.

Someone had crept up on us.

I shouted a warning.

The men rushed to my side.

"Watch for the pony," the Lieutenant yelled. "Someone is trying to steal it."

Sure enough, a convict had crept to where Patch was tethered. He tried to lead her away. As the men came bearing down on him, he bared his teeth and stood ready to do battle.

Before the convict's fists could land, Lieutenant Collins hit him over the head with his musket.

The convict moaned and crumpled to the ground.

A deathly silence followed.

"You've killed him," Margaret shrieked.

We stood there, too horrified to speak.

But no, the convict sat up nursing his head. Abel set about tying the thief's hands behind his back. My Master stood over him waving his staff.

"Not again," the convict whimpered. "Don't hit me again."

"Why not?" my Master said sternly. "You were stealing our pony. You deserve to be punished."

"I'm hungry," the convict whimpered. "I ain't had nothing in me stomach all week. Me rations were all stole. I need vittles or I'll die."

125

Poor Patch. She might have a running sore on her right front leg and limp very badly, but she does not deserve to be anyone's dinner.

I glanced at my Master. Even though I know him to be the kindest soul in Port Jackson, his next move astonished even me. "Let the villain go," he told Abel. "He can no longer harm us." This was the truth, as the fellow could no more fight anyone than swim back to England.

Abel shook his head. "He'll only steal someone else's goods." And to the convict, "You knows what happens to horse thieves? They strings them up." He turned to us. "How about we teach this scoundrel a lesson?"

At this the convict set up such a hue and cry, I had to remind myself that he was not the only one who was famished. My Master's sunken eyes and sharp cheekbones showed how hungry he was. Still he insisted that we free the man, arguing that lack of food forces folk into committing foolish crimes.

Abel reluctantly did as my Master suggested.

Now the convict thanked us over and over again. "Listen my poor fellow," my Master said. "If you do not want us to take you back to the militia – and they will surely string you up – you had best be on your way."

The convict cried his thanks. Before you could say Port Jackson, he had disappeared into the bush.

My Master sighed aloud. "This is not a good sign of what we will find in Sydney Cove," he told the Lieutenant. "Have we sunk into mutiny already?"

The Lieutenant shook his head and could give no proper answer.

In the morning we farewelled Abel and Margaret. The Lieutenant and ourselves were travelling to Sydney Cove, they to Rose Hill. But not before I asked Margaret to report to Sarah that I am well, but missing her most dreadfully.

Margaret had seen me writing in my journal, and she wanted to know why I did not send Sarah a letter? Most reluctantly, I explained that Sarah could not read.

"Nor me," Margaret said gravely. "It is a grave fault that must surely be remedied. One day you must show us how."

I promised her that I would, and at the very first chance.

We went on our way. Soon the track grew wider. But the way was so churned up Patch's front legs sank into the mud. Several times we had to stop in order to help her out.

I would have thought that we had had quite enough

adventures. But there were more to come. A mile further, the track narrowed so much we were forced to walk in single file. Winston led our group. I was just behind.

Suddenly something long and brown slithered across the path.

The creature raised its head. It was ready to strike.

Remembering Old Tom's warnings about venomous snakes, I let out a mighty yell.

Winston leapt into the air and fell backwards. My Master held up his stick and brought it down on the wicked creature. He struck it often enough to kill it.

As we stood there inspecting the remains, my heart thumped as if it might jump out of my chest. My Master stood there, breathing heavily. Then he turned to me saying, "Well done, Scheherazade. Without your quick action, Winston might now be dead. He owes you his life."

He waited for Winston to thank me – which I thought that he did most grudgingly – and we continued on our way.

Now we were passing cleared areas where timber had been recently felled. Sitting amongst the stumps were one-room huts. They had not been there the last time I came through.

Emily's chest was so much stronger. Riding on Winston's shoulders, she could not stop asking questions. As we walked my Master explained to her how wattle walls are hung onto a frame, then covered with mud and finished with a thin coat of pipe-clay.

We walked another half-hour before reaching Sydney Cove. There we came to the Governor's house. My Master had planned to call in to deliver certain tidings from Rose Hill. But so many people were waiting to see Governor Phillip, he decided to return a little later.

We were most impressed with the Governor's two-story dwelling. It is built with the first bricks from Brickfields. My Master pointed to the gardens surrounding the house where many fruit trees and vegetables had been planted. He thought they set a great example to this colony.

A little further on, we came to the officer's house in which we were to live. Here half a dozen children, the bigger tugging the smaller by their hands, hurried towards us. Half-naked and with weepy eyes, running noses and protruding bellies, they pointed to their mouths, demanding that we give them food. Though we are desperately short ourselves, my Master handed them the last of our johnny-cakes. Then he shooed them away.

I would have liked to ask him what he expected us

to eat, but one look at his grave face and I did not dare.

I set about unpacking and making the room as comfortable as possible. Though Winston hardly opens his mouth to me except when absolutely necessary, he carried the heavier packages into the hut. For this I was grateful. But he always makes it clear that any friendship between us is out of the question. As this is only to be expected, why does it bother me so much?

This hut is quite superior to Master Dodd's house in Rose Hill. From the doorway I can see the storehouses and then out to the harbour. If a sail appears in the harbour, I might be the first to sight it.

Outside our door there is a patch cleared of tree stumps that will make an excellent vegetable garden. I intend to dig it over and ask my Master for seeds.

Travelling even the short distance between here and Rose Hill is tiresome. I hope that we will stay here awhile, even though I miss Sarah most sorely.

Wednesday, 19th May

I am writing everything down so that you, Edward, will know every place I have seen and how I presently live.

Sydney Cove is grey and scrubby. It looks out into the harbour and across at the hills on the other side. Many of the convicts' huts have been built on rocks. They are so ramshackle their foundations must cling like limpets or a strong wind will surely send them into the water.

But we are more fortunate. This officer's house where I now live is far more permanent. Four sturdy wooden posts have been set in the ground to support a grooved timber frame. The walls are vertical slabs, the cracks filled with mud. The roof is made of timber shingles fixed to the battens with wooden pegs. Our chimney is built from the same brick as the Governor's house. I am very proud of our door. It has leather hinges so it can open and close more easily.

The bush behind our hut is grey and scrubby. At night, our candles and oil lamps attract moths big as birds and monstrous black beetles that go clickety-clack against our walls. There are also dozens of possums and large furry bats. My Master says that because no one farms or owns this land, all animals are free to roam wherever they might wish.

First thing this morning, I opened my eyes to a giant black spider sitting on the pallet beside my head. As the spider scuttled away, I shrieked and sprang to my feet.

My Master raised his head, his eyes fuzzy with sleep. "What's the matter?"

I burst into tears. Bad enough to wake to such a monster, now I had incurred my Master's wrath.

"There is so much here that frightens me," I finally managed.

He reached out a comforting hand. "Do not allow yourself to get so upset. Nothing here is permanent. We will not be staying here forever."

At least the weather is kind. Though it is almost winter, the mid-day sun warms us. My Master spent all day and most of the night in the hospital. This hospital is little more than a dispensary where he treats the sick with herbs and much use of leeches and purging. He tells me that he has not been forced to saw off any limbs. I suppose that is some comfort for having to care for his patients in what is, after all, only a tent.

Winston disappeared in the direction of the barracks almost as soon as we arrived. The militia practise marching to the fife and drum. They have no ammunition, nor little to do except shoulder their muskets and try to look as warlike as possible.

As for myself, I have many chores. I had to fetch water from the Tank Stream twice today. It is so far to walk when Emily is not well and I must piggyback her.

Thursday, 20 May

Emily's reading goes well. She can recognize many words. She tells me that she would like to read the Bible. But my Master tells me that in all of Port Jackson we have only one Bible and one prayer book. Perchance this is no great loss. Those books have many long words, and her reading is not yet good enough.

Once her lessons are over, I must find new ways to keep her occupied. This is not difficult. People still go about their business, though with a little less willingness than if they had full bellies. How we long to sight a sail. Everyone thinks that any loud noise, such as thunder or a tree being felled, is the cannon announcing a ship's arrival. They race in great excitement towards the wharves only to be just as quickly disappointed.

There is a hill not far from here where we get an excellent view of the harbour. It will be our favourite place to settle. When Emily's lessons are over, and the housework done, we will come here to gaze out to the harbour. Emily longs to be the first to sight a sail.

This morning we set off to explore this colony. Turning left we walked past the storehouse – it has a canvas roof and timber walls – and set off towards the wharves. As we got closer, the path became so steep it was hard not to slip and fall. On the wharf, a group of men were casting lines. Several small fish lay between them. They must have thought that we had come to steal their catch because they shouted at us to stay away. As we took off, I heard them quarrelling amongst themselves.

My Master reports that lack of food makes people tired and irritable. Perchance he is right. If I ask Emily to put on her boots or her cap, she weeps and refuses.

We hurried inland. From here we could see more forest. Dark mountains hover on the horizon. I shiver whenever I look at them. They are a curious colour – purple or maybe dark blue – like nothing I could ever have imagined, not even in my dreams. Surely dragons and one-eyed monsters lurk in those ridges and valleys.

As we hurried towards the river, we heard banging from the forge, soldiers drilling at the barracks to the fife and drum, people calling to each other as they carried water to their huts.

Soon we came to a timber bridge. Here a crowd, dressed in the most ragged excuse I have ever seen for clothes, was quickly gathering. What I first thought was a prayer gathering turned out to be a seaman perched on a tree shouting, "You tells us why the Governor gives as much vittles to the convicts as to us freemen. Most of them are no better than Indians, and don't deserve the same rations…"

A fellow, tall and brawny and almost certainly a convict, stepped out from the crowd to snarl, "Who says?"

"I does!" the seaman retorted, though he was thin as a whippet and would barely reach the other's chest.

The convict pulled the seaman to the ground and set

about teaching him a lesson. Several onlookers objected, and a free-for-all broke out. To add to the confusion, some militiamen standing by decided to subdue the crowd with the ends of their muskets.

Emily and I watched all this from a safe distance. When the fight seemed to be heading our way, I piggybacked Emily past the male convict huts towards the barracks. She has long wished to visit Winston. Instead we ran into Mistress Isabella Lawson who had sailed with me on the *Lady Penrhyn*.

The good mistress greeted me most warmly. Then she wanted to know how Sarah was? And what Government Farm was like? And was it true that we were living there like kings? And did we really eat six big meals a day? And when would we start sending food back to Sydney Cove?

Before I could explain that things were not so much better in Rose Hill, we were joined by Mistress Jane Chapman also bound for the barracks. She carried a basket – it had a fishy smell – it was probably for someone in the militia, though she would not say who this was. Jane has a well-known weakness for rum. I was sure that she intended trading her basket's contents for something more potent.

The women set about gossiping. First they spoke

about the convict Mary Bryant who had recently escaped from Port Jackson by boat.

Then the women moved on to Governor Phillip. Seems that our Governor, though an excellent seaman and administrator, had never obtained a post worthy of his talents. Isabella thought it had something to do with him missing a front tooth. Jane sighed wistfully. "It's said that he earns 500 pounds for running this colony. What I could do with that money…"

I said, "Even a thousand guineas will not buy you food where there is none."

"Lizzie's right!" Jane exclaimed.

By now Emily had heard enough. She kicked my ribs, insisting that I go into the barracks and find Winston. I did so reluctantly. Has not Sarah always warned me to stay away from places where men gather?

To my relief Winston saw us soon we walked into the barracks. He offered to carry Emily home. She is always thrilled to see him. As she managed to chatter all the way there, I could tell that she was breathing more easily.

Friday, 21st May

Today Emily refused to do her lessons. I told my Master and he said that we should take two days' holiday. I carried a stick in one hand, and Emily clung to the other. Together, we have been exploring the colony.

Walking helps us ignore our rumbling bellies. Governor Phillip has further reduced our rations. Now one week's food for each person is a kilo of pork and a kilo of rice. We must eke this out with whatever else we can find. Many are eating rats, birds, possums, even snakes. Some have managed to grow a few vegetables. I have planted seeds – potatoes, lettuce, parsnips and carrots – in a wooden box that my Master found for me.

My Master is fortunate in that vegetables are offered to him in exchange for his services. Yesterday he came home with an excellent cabbage, some half-grown carrots and six potatoes – though these were green and gave us diarrhoea. My Master says folk complain that they are too weak to do a proper day's work. He tells me that if an officer invites another to dinner, that the visitor cannot come unless he brings his own food.

From what I have seen, there is little in this settlement to admire. As each day drags by, people must pull their belts a little tighter. Chests are hollow. Arms and legs are like sticks. Hair falls out in clumps. Teeth become shaky.

Hunger sinks a person's eyes into their sockets. Hunger gives even the most hardened criminal a wistful expression. If anyone carries a little extra flesh, he or she is accused of stealing food. At the same time many women are heavy with child. It seems that by next summer, instead of reaping oats and corn and potatoes as we should be doing, we shall be birthing babies.

Not that the children look any better than their parents. Ragged, lice-ridden and with swollen bellies, many have dreadful coughs and running noses. Some are orphans. These have formed small gangs of thieves as excellent at their trade as any in London. But word has gone out that Surgeon Russell has food. Each time I walk outside, I am approached by groups of children who beg and beg most piteously. I feel very sorry for them. But I have nothing to spare.

Saturday, 22nd May

Yesterday as we walked along the shore, I noticed folk gathering shellfish. So this morning at low tide, Emily and I walked along the shore. I used a sharp knife to prise oysters and mussels from the rocks. Emily pulls a face whenever I insist that she eat her share. I tell her that if she swallows very quickly, she will begin to enjoy them.

When she grows tired, or begins to wheeze, I carry her on my back. Thankfully these last two days she has been well enough to walk. The furthest we have gone is the observatory at Point Maskelyne.

I had heard that Lieutenant William Dawes was given the task of studying the southern stars. I think that he must get rather lonely, because no sooner did he glimpse us, than he raced outside to invite us in to admire his delicate instruments. He told us how Governor Phillip thought this project so important he even spared the Lieutenant some of his own precious nails. The Lieutenant made the octagonal roof revolve – they are panels made of white painted canvas –

explaining that this was so every part of the night sky might be studied.

Emily demanded to know if he had built this observatory himself. He smiled and shook his head. "A gang of marines and convicts helped me complete this in just four months."

"Why such a rush?" I asked.

His smile grew broader – he seems very proud of all he has achieved. He said, "Very shortly a comet is expected to streak over the southern skies."

We thanked him and set off towards the cliffs nearby. Looking down at craggy rocks covered in spindly salt bush made my head spin and I quickly moved away.

We turned back towards the Tank Stream. We smelt it long before we reached it. Even in Blackfriars or East Smithfield in London it is hard to find such a mess of garbage and human excrement. People have emptied their chamber pots along the banks and into the stream. The air is black with flies. My Master has instructed me to only collect water from upstream. Though this water is sweeter, it means that I must walk nearly a mile both there and back.

Last night I dared question my Master's instructions. I said that it would be far easier for me to collect water from where others go.

His gaze grew inward as he sucked on his empty pipe. At last he said, "I have noticed that those who drink that water often become sick. Best that you walk a little further."

One more task to add to all my others. He has also instructed me to carry enough water to bathe Emily. At first I objected, saying that the sea soaks her well enough when we go looking for oysters.

"But she is still in her clothes," he replied, "and so much salt cannot be good for her delicate skin. I think a bath would do us all good."

I have calculated that I must bring home at least four buckets of water and then set about heating them. When I reminded my Master that we had no soap, he said that we could scrape ourselves with a tin spoon, and add crushed tea-tree leaves to the water. He says that this will soothe our chapped skins.

More and more he reminds me of my own father. Papa was also a hard, though very fair, taskmaster. Lately if I try to recall what he looked like, instead my Master's face comes into my mind. Edward, is your memory any better than mine? If ever I try to picture your face, you stay constantly six years old. Do you have fair hair and blue eyes like myself? Are you tall –

I mean as tall as a ten-year-old boy can grow – or are you short like me? No matter how often I tell myself that one day we will be together, when you are half a world away, it is too hard to believe this.

Tonight, preparing that bath tired me immensely. Perchance it is hunger that weakens my body and sinks my spirits this low.

Sunday, 23rd May

This morning I went upstream to fetch more water. Emily was wheezing too much to walk so I piggybacked her most of the way. My Master instructs me to never leave her alone, not even in the hut, as some very strange folk roam this colony.

Emily has long wanted to visit the school. So after our mid-day dinner of a little rice and pease pudding, we set off in that direction. We heard the children long before we saw them. Camped under a copse of river gums, they were reciting "The Lord's Prayer".

We introduced ourselves to their teacher Mistress Isabella Rosson – a matron in her mid twenties with a gaunt face and a longish nose and chin. Her smile is kind. I think that she would be quite pretty were she not half-starved.

She brought us to a raggedy group of about a dozen children aged between five and ten. All with watery eyes and snotty noses, hair that has never known a good brushing and protruding bellies. They were as interested in Emily as she was in them. They have no chalk or slates. These children write with sharp sticks in the dust. Mistress Rosson set them all, Emily too, to writing "The cat on the mat" and "God bless our new home".

As the children worked, we gossiped awhile. She spoke of the children in her class, saying, "True, they are hungry. But the air is fresh. There are no dangerous wild animals and they are not forced into becoming chimney sweeps or thieves. These children have a far better chance of surviving than if they had stayed in England."

I said, "Will all the children born in this colony attend your school?"

"Who knows," she said softly. "It is hard to learn when there are no books, no slates, and no roof. Whenever it rains, I have no choice but to send them home."

Then she very politely told us that it was time to go, as the children still had much to do. As I walked away, we could hear them repeating an old counting rhyme I had learned back home:

> *One, two, three, four,*
> *Mary at the cottage door.*
> *Five, six, seven, eight,*
> *Mary at the cottage gate.*

We were almost home when a man darted out from the scrub. I was piggybacking Emily, and we had such a fright, she nearly fell off my back. To my astonishment it was Simple Sam, and he was smiling as if delighted that he had finally found me. He was followed by a small group of children who were busy throwing stones and copying his strange gestures.

He gave them as much attention as he would a swarm of flies. "Sam hungry," he cried and made lots more sounds that made little sense. In the end I realized that he has been expelled from Rose Hill. He is now wandering around Sydney Cove without a morsel of food to bless himself.

"If you jump out on people like that," I scolded him, "they will think you are trying to steal from them." But

I do not think that he understood because he kept on smiling, his arms and legs moving like cartwheels.

Emily was so frightened she started to cry. I hurried her away, praying that he would not follow. I looked back, and he was still talking and waving his limbs while the children poked him with sticks and threw more stones.

I cannot understand my Master. He is so caring for the sick yet he has no tolerance for Simple Sam. What is it that turns my Master against him?

Back home I boiled a small fish with the last of the carrots for supper. Even Emily – and she eats very little – is hungry. I wish that I owned a fishing-net. Perchance I could find some string to use as a line. What if I fashioned a hook from one of our nails? To this I could attach a chicken feather as bait.

Chicken feathers! When Mama was alive, she would dye them with vegetable peelings to decorate Lady Jane's splendid hats.

Edward, how far away England seems. How I hate this dull bush that surrounds us. What I would give to see soft hills, misty with rain, and the little cottage with the thatched roof where we were born and I grew up.

I tell myself that Mama is in Heaven, and Papa too. That they keep watch over you and me and this is why

I am still alive. But sometimes it is hard to believe this.

My Master is watching me write. He asks me every day for a full report of our activities. He wants to know where we have walked and what we have seen. I am careful to tell him everything. But I have not mentioned Simple Sam. I know that he will order me to keep Emily well away from someone he thinks is dangerous.

Tonight I have a toothache and it is hard to concentrate on my journal. I had asked my Master to look into my mouth. He says that a left back tooth is totally rotten. He will have to pull it out. I asked him to leave this for later, but he says that the longer this tooth stays, the more painful it will be. Before the extraction, he has promised to give me a tot of rum to lessen the pain.

Monday, 24th May

Winston has borrowed one of the rowboats. He tells me that he intends to spend all day fishing. He did not invite anyone to go with him. I thought this most selfish of him, but was hardly surprised. Mostly Winston only thinks about himself. Yet it is a shame that he did not take Emily, even for a little while. Surely the boat's gentle movement would bring more colour into her cheeks? Even if he does catch a fish, it will be tasteless as we have no salt.

I hear that there is no salt in this colony and that the Governor has ordered two large vats of seawater to be boiled into crystals.

This morning, the fireplace needed brushing. As I was sweeping the hearth, soot fell down the chimney onto my face so that I looked like an Indian. I was sorely annoyed but Emily giggled so much, in the end I had to smile, even though the cap I wore had been clean and my other was not yet dry.

Emily had demanded another holiday from schoolwork. As she was breathing more easily and seemed willing to walk, we set off along the coast. Hoping to find more shellfish I carried a knife and our oldest bucket. This bucket is no longer waterproof, but works well as a basket.

A mild day with a light wind, and we wandered further east than we had intended. Soon we were met by a terrible stench. We kept on walking and eventually we reached a low hill entirely composed of empty seashells. Suddenly I thought that perhaps we were standing on the end result of thousands of dinners.

By now the stink was so bad we had to hold our nostrils so as not to vomit. On the far side of the hill a horrible sight greeted us. A score or so of dead natives lay there, all covered in terrible sores. Their arms and legs were bent into unnatural positions. Black flies swarmed over the bodies. One corpse – this was a female – held a baby in her arms.

Aghast, I clapped my hands over Emily's eyes and hurried her away.

My Master had mentioned that smallpox, cholera and influenza have swept through the Indians. This is the result. It would seem that the poor things are too sick to even bury their dead.

All thoughts of gathering shellfish forgotten, we rushed back along the track that led to our house.

Tuesday, 25th May

Today while we were out walking, we were met by more upset.

Simple Sam – this time surrounded by more than teasing children. An angry crowd had gathered around him. "Where's the child?" someone yelled.

"Tell us what you did to her, or we'll string you to the nearest tree…"

"He's a kidnapper an' a murderer. He only pretends to be simple…"

"String him up on Gallows Hill…"

I could sense Sam's distress. Even someone as foolish as Sam can grasp hatred when it is solely directed towards him.

I approached an old crone – she seemed one of the ringleaders – to ask what was happening. Her witch's chin bobbed up and down. "Mistress Mullen's child, a girl of less'en four years, has disappeared. She was seen talking with him," and she pointed accusingly at Sam.

I said, "Has no one gone to look for the child?"

The crone shook her head. Just then I glimpsed Winston edging around the crowd. Pulling Emily by her hand – she protesting mightily – I set off after him.

We caught up with him outside our hut where I quickly explained what was happening. Then I pleaded with him to help me rescue the poor fellow.

He shook his head and went to walk away. I clung to his arm, hotly insisting, "But you must. Sam is totally harmless. It is only his speech and the way he cannot control his limbs that make folk think he is dangerous. You always talk about how people are judged unfairly. How they are transported and even hanged for the crime of being poor. Now you will let them murder Simple Sam for no fault of his own? Actions must suit brave words," and I burst into angry tears.

He flushed scarlet and stammered, "Are you accusing me of cowardice?"

But I had gone too far. I would gain nothing from making Winston angry. "No," I cried. "But you cannot let them hang an innocent man."

I pushed Emily into his arms and ran back to where Sam was facing an increasingly hostile crowd.

There being no way I could protect him without turning the crowd's anger onto myself, I followed Sam.

They dragged him all the way to Gallows Hill. Here we were met by a terrible stink of rotting corpses. Several bodies swung in the wind. Black crows wheeled lazily around them. While I watched in dismay, the crowd pushed Sam towards an empty spot on the gallows.

Suddenly a slight figure, hat hiding his hair, handkerchief tied over his face and carrying a musket, walked towards the crowd. I thought that I recognized that slim build. Then I decided that this must be my imagination. Had not Winston refused to help Sam in any way?

The masked figure pointed his musket at the ringleaders. They came to an abrupt stop. The masked man shouted, "First this villain must be p–properly tried in a c–court of law."

That stammer! Winston? As I stared in disbelief, someone in the crowd yelled, "We tried him enough."

"D–Do not make me fire," Winston threatened.

"Ignore him," someone yelled from the sidelines. "He ain't got no shot. There ain't no shot in all o' Port Jackson."

Winston swung his musket around. "Shall I prove to you otherwise?" And amidst much muttering and cursing from a crowd after blood, and not too choosy

152

as to whose it might be, he grabbed hold of Sam. Then he led Sam to me.

Still pointing his musket at the crowd, he helped me pull Sam behind a clump of trees. Then we took off towards home, dragging Sam behind us.

Emily had been lying on her pallet, but as soon as she glimpsed Sam, she shrieked in fright. We had to pull him back outside so she would no longer be so terrified. I cried, "Where can we hide him?"

Meanwhile poor Sam was gibbering and shaking enough to start an earth tremor. I reached out to comfort him, but even in such a life-threatening situation it was hard to stand too close as he stank so badly.

Winston shook his head and glared at me. I could tell he was wondering why he had gone to so much trouble to save this poor scrap of humanity.

I cried, "He cannot stay where your papa will see him. He will surely deliver Sam back to the crowd."

Winston wiped sweat off his face and grunted. Though this meant that we must leave Emily on her own – and this was strictly against my Master's orders – he decided that we should take Sam upstream. Dragging the poor fellow after us, we set off into the scrub, finally coming to the place where I collect water. There we found a decent clump of river gums and told Sam to hide behind them. The poor thing's teeth were chattering with fear. But I do not think that he fully understood the danger he was in, because when I looked back, he was in full view of anyone coming the other way. Arms and legs making windmills in the air, he was staring piteously after us.

Back in the hut, Emily had fallen asleep. Winston handed me the three small fish he had caught that morning. I set about gutting and cleaning them. After I thanked him on poor Sam's behalf, I said, "Your papa is such a good kind man. Why does he show Sam no mercy?"

Winston took a long while to answer. I watched him wander around the hut, first to stare at his sleeping sister, then to peer absentmindedly through the open door. He shook his head as if it to clear it. Only then did he sigh and say, "Lizzie, this goes back to when I was no more than ten years old. In Cornwall where we lived, the village idiot stole a child. This child was later found murdered."

I asked him, "Who was that child?"

Tears filled his eyes. He turned away before muttering, "Her name was Elizabeth. They called her Lizzie. Just like you. On the fifteenth day of next month she would have turned eighteen. Lizzie was my elder sister and we loved her most dearly. She had b–blue eyes, fair hair, and she was thin and small. Some might even say that she looked a little like you."

I felt the blood run into my cheeks. How could I have been so rude and unfeeling? Yet it was if a veil had been lifted from my eyes. This explained why my Master could not tolerate Sam.

Then I cried, "But Simple Sam is different. He has not enough strength in his arms and legs to kidnap anybody. The poor fellow is just hungry."

Winston rubbed the back of his neck and did not answer. We listened to the birds carol in the trees outside. Truly it must be easier to be a bird, I thought tiredly. Easier not to see and understand all these terrible things that are happening around us. And not to have to think about them.

My mind in a whirl, I continued scaling the fish.

I heard Winston clear his throat. I glanced up and to my astonishment he said, "Lizzie, I have not been kind to you. Not kind at all." He paused for a moment to rub his eyes. I gulped. I did not know what to say. I was not ready for such an unexpected change. But he went on. "I had already lost a mother and a sister. To become close to anyone else…" He shook his head.

This explained why Winston was careful to never get close to another girl – even though she was but a poor convict and not actually related. And to add to his unhappiness, I bore the same name, even looked a little like his beloved sister. This explained so much that had puzzled me before.

At first I could find nothing to say. Then, "But… But you are good to Emily…"

"Emily is too often unwell." He left the rest unsaid. "Can you find it in your heart to forgive me?"

I saw that he was waiting for my answer, so I swallowed and murmured, "Even though I am a girl and a convict?"

"Even so." His voice was gruff. "So … can we now be friends?"

"Friends forever," I said. I put down my knife, and we clasped hands.

Just then Emily woke and demanded to know if the fearsome man was still around. We assured her that he had gone and that she was absolutely safe. Then we made her promise not to mention him to her papa.

Shortly after my Master came home and told us that the whole colony was abuzz. A simpleton had kidnapped a girl child. Before he could be punished, he had been whisked away by a masked stranger. Now neither simpleton nor rescuer could be found.

Winston glanced a warning at me. Together we asked enough questions about my Master's work in the dispensary to divert his attention.

After we finished our suppers, my Master gave me a stiff swig of rum. Then he commanded me to sit on a stool and open my mouth. He reached inside with a special tool he uses for such operations. Enough to say that the tooth was so rotten it snapped in two as he pulled it out. It took him a long time to remove the pieces. Then he swabbed the wound with a clean rag dipped in tea-tree tincture.

I bled all over my bodice and the pain is most severe. My cheek is swollen to double its size. Even if we did have more to eat, my jaw would be too sore to chew on it.

But we are so short of food. My arms and legs are nothing but skin and bone. And no matter how often I wet my hair to smooth it, the texture is coarse and brittle. Also, my fingernails splinter too easily and my belly is as swollen as if I had just eaten a whole chicken. The others look much the same. My Master says lack of food causes our bodies to grow old before their time.

Though it is very late, he has kindly allowed me a

little extra oil for the lantern so I can record today's events. I think that he likes to see me filling this journal, though he never asks to read what I have written. If he did, I do not know what I could say. Perchance there are things in here that will offend him.

Wednesday, 26th May

My Master left shortly before sunrise for the dispensary. He told me that he would not be home until well after sunset. Not long after, I heard shouting. I went outside to see a group of men vanishing along the track leading inland. Back inside I stared at Winston. The same question was in both our eyes. What was happening to Simple Sam?

Winston pulled on a shirt and set off after the crowd.

I had much to do. But while I fed Emily a little porridge made from boiled rice, my knees trembled with anxiety. Poor Sam. What was happening to him? An hour later, Winston returned. He did not have to speak. His face told me everything.

I sank onto the stool and closed my eyes. I knew Sam was dead. My mind's eye saw his poor body swinging in the breeze on Gallows Hill. Then I remembered the stolen child. "Did they find her?"

Winston slowly nodded. "This is the terrible thing," he said. "The girl is alive and well. The mother had drunk so much rum she had totally forgotten where her child was."

Suddenly Emily started to cough and wheeze. Before I could rush to her aid, she had thrown up all her breakfast. I was about to scold her for wasting food and for not vomiting into the bucket when I realized that she was fighting for air. Winston helped her clean the vomit off herself. Meanwhile, as my Master had instructed, I filled a pan with hot water, and poured into it a few drops of my Master's mixture that he makes from crushed tea-tree leaves. We held Emily's head over the fumes. This seemed to relieve the wheezing. But her cheeks and lips were so drained of blood they seemed almost blue.

Because I could see that this attack was a very bad one, and would probably last a long time, I asked Winston to go to the dispensary and bring his papa home.

Half an hour later, my Master was examining Emily very thoroughly. He decided that a chill had settled on her chest, and that we must watch over her every minute. "Lizzie," he said, "I have too many sick patients to care for and I cannot stay. I have every confidence in you and I charge you with Emily's complete care."

I gulped and nodded.

Now we are entirely alone. Winston had to return to the barracks, but he has promised to be back before nightfall. In the meantime Emily is running a fever. Her little body feels as if it might burn up. I write in this journal between wiping her face with a wet cloth, sponging her body and trying to force a little water between her lips. But she cannot hold anything down. She is really very sick. When Winston came home and saw how poorly she was, he ran to fetch his papa.

Emily is sleeping, though still very restless. I write in my journal while I wait for the others to return.

Thursday, 27th May

Emily is still sick. My Master and I stayed up most of the night trying to bring her fever down. This morning I was too tired to manage any housework. Shortly after sunrise my Master returned to the hospital leaving Emily in my care. Though I sponged her body and dribbled water between her parched lips, she is no better.

Winston came home at mid-day. He offered to look after her while I went to fill the water buckets.

The weather is cool and dry. What rain we had came at the wrong time. So much wet in February and so little now. The crops are not flourishing. Even my little seeds refuse to sprout.

As I walked along the track hardly anyone was about. Then I remembered Winston saying that people have become too weak and dispirited to tackle any serious chores. Still, it is surprising to meet so few folk on what is usually a busy path.

Halfway to the river, I came across Mistress Jane Chapman carrying two laden buckets. She set them down long enough to inquire about the Surgeon and his family's health. She was most concerned when I told her how ill Emily was. She quickly offered to look after her if I was needed elsewhere. She is a good kind woman, even if she does reek of rum. "If ships don't come soon," she said at last, "we will all surely die."

I said, "How do people manage?"

"Why, many are half-mad with starvation."

I stared at her in dismay. "Does this mean they kill themselves?"

"One poor soul has done as much. She ate her entire week's ration as soon as she received it, and died shortly of overeating." She laughed as if she found this most amusing.

I have noticed that the worse our conditions become, the more people must laugh or give way under the strain. A bone stripped of all meat is a "Sydney Cove steak". An empty dish is a "Port Jackson stew". A vegetable peeling is a "Botany Bay pineapple".

Mistress Jane said, "It seems that this poor woman ate uncooked rice and it expanded and exploded her belly."

My eyes widened in alarm. "Surely not everyone is so crazed by hunger?"

She stopped smiling. "I know of other women who sacrifice their own rations so their children will not starve. Others who use every wile and trick to steal their partner's food. Some are said to even eat snails, spiders, grass, leaves, dirt…"

Though I was in a great hurry to get back to Emily, I could not help cutting in, "Surely things are not so bad on Norfolk Island. Perhaps we should all have sailed with Captain Ross?"

She chuckled. "The governor finds Ross most argumentative and disagreeable. But the man's luck is in. On Norfolk Island there are many green turtles and mutton-birds to eat, though their taste is fishy and horrid."

"When you are hungry, taste does not matter," I said dryly, and we went our different ways.

But she has left me much to think about. What a sorry state we are in. We have waited so long for the Second Fleet to arrive. I am beginning to think that they are all lost at sea. Only Governor Phillip's wise rule stops us from descending into mutiny and death.

These and other sad thoughts filling my mind, I collected my buckets and set off for home. All the way I told myself that Emily will be so much better. That when I walk in, she will raise her head and smile.

Winston met me at the door, tears rolling down his cheeks. In the short time I had been gone Emily had fallen into a deep trance. I listened to her chest. Her breath is so forced, it is doubtful that she can survive. Winston has gone to fetch my Master. No matter what is happening in the hospital or how much he is needed, he should, he *must* be here with Emily.

Friday, 28th May

Emily is still no better. She cannot breathe. Her wheeze grows louder by the hour. Both her papa and her brother sit by her pallet. Though an icy blast comes through the open window, we have made the room warm as possible. My Master continues with his tea-tree mixtures in an attempt to ease her chest. So far nothing does.

Just before sunset there was an unexpected burst of thunder. I raced outside. Was this the cannon telling us that a sail has been sighted? From here I could see other folk racing towards the shore. I stayed there looking out to sea. But the horizon was empty. I saw nothing. Nothing.

Saturday, 29th May

Emily drew her last breath in the early hours of this morning. Now her dear face is at last peaceful. She looks as if she is about to open her eyes and talk to us. I try to draw comfort from knowing that she and her dear mama have been reunited. Though her papa does not weep, his eyes seem to burn holes in their sockets.

But nothing will console Winston. He cries and cries. He suffers doubly now that he has lost both his mama and two sisters. I feel so sorry for him and for his papa, and for myself too...

I wish I knew a way of making us feel better.

I spent most of today sitting in Emily's favourite spot overlooking the harbour. This way I can pretend that she is still with me.

These last days have passed in a dream. Each time I leave the hut to fetch water and firewood, I expect to come home to find Emily waiting for me.

Everywhere I look, everything my eyes alight upon, reminds me of her. This house is filled with her presence: her clothes, her hobbyhorse that we carried all the way from Rose Hill, her doll, her wooden top. I keep on waiting for her to run inside and call to me.

We buried her under a stand of red gums not far from here. Winston fashioned a small wooden cross and wrote her name upon it. He says that shortly he will shape a tombstone. Then he will carve on it:

EMILY MARY RUSSELL
(b. September 1785 – d. May 1790)

Her body may lie there, but her memory will stay with me forever.

Today both the Surgeon and Winston returned to their duties. I think that for them this is best. But I do not know what to do with myself. Whereas before I was always so busy, always had too much to do, suddenly I find myself wandering in aimless circles. Tears roll down my cheeks. I cannot stop crying. I weep for all the people I have lost. The tears never seem to end. I cannot believe that I still have so much crying left in me.

Also, and this seems so selfish while Emily still lies warm in her grave, hunger forms a hollow in my belly. Hunger makes me so weary I could sleep away the nights and half the days. But when I sleep, I dream. And then my dreams are plagued with images of freshly baked bread. Creamy milk and butter from Mama's cow. Mutton pies covered in gravy. New season peas, beans and apples. Wild strawberries and berries plucked from the hedgerows.

I wish that I were not so tired. All I want to do is sleep.

Tuesday, 1st June

We have no food. My Master sent me to gather shellfish. I walked as far as the Lieutenant Dawes' observatory. This being a very long way from our hut, it took me two hours to get there. But when I knocked on Lieutenant Dawes' door, no one was about.

The last time Emily and I came here, I had noticed how the house was not far from a cliff. Below it was a wide band of rocks. They were the kind of rocks where oysters flourish.

Perchance this was not the best time to go looking for shellfish. The wind was high, the tide only half out. I felt weak from too much hunger and despair.

The cliff face was covered in pale green succulents. Hanging onto them to steady myself, I slid down to where the sea hit the rocks. On their inner side, the sides not facing out to sea, I could see rich oyster beds. I think there were enough to keep us in food for several days. What I had not realized was how sharp those rocks were. Or how hard it would be to balance myself on the rock's slippery surface. Or how wild was the sea.

I was reaching forward to loosen a fat oyster when a white-crested wave swept me off my perch. The wave carried my bucket and knife out to sea, and tried to make me follow. Just in time I managed to cling to a rock where I waited for the wave to subside.

My hands scratched and bleeding, I slid further along the shelf to look for my tools. No sign of the knife. But about ten yards out, the bucket bobbed along the waves.

Tears rolled down my cheeks. Yet another calamity amongst so many. Both knife and bucket would be missed. I had no means of replacing them. My Master would be angry.

I turned to climb back to the top of the cliff. But the way up was much harder than coming down. Halfway, my foot slipped and sent an avalanche of mud and rocks tumbling into the sea.

I glanced down. That was a mistake. My stomach lurched. I swayed and felt dizzy. Waves poured over the rock where I had just stood.

I swayed a little more. One more moment, and I was about to fall…

I closed my eyes and waited for my heart to stop pounding.

Only two more steps, I told myself, and you will be safe.

I grasped a salt-bush growing at the very edge of the cliff. To my horror, the branch was too brittle to hold up my weight. It snapped in two. My only luck was that my other hand still clung to a protruding ledge. But I could go no further. Meanwhile, dozens of seagulls wheeled above my head. Thinking I had come to raid their nests for eggs, they cawed angrily at me.

Only one more move, I told myself, and you will be safe.

But I had not an ounce of energy left within me. Not even enough to save myself from falling, nor to prevent myself from being dashed against those rocks.

Instead I hung there, poised between heaven and hell, and without that last effort needed to haul myself into safety. Another moment and I would fall. Another moment and I would be dead. And perhaps this would not be so bad. Then I would no longer have to live with hunger and despair as my constant companions…

I have heard that in the few moments before people drown, their whole life passes before their eyes. Something like that happened to me.

Edward, you may find this hard to believe, but as in a dream I saw myself as a small child with you running beside me, and coming home to a warm supper and loving parents. I saw Mama and Papa become ill and die. Then myself as an apprentice, racing along the streets of London. I saw the years in Newgate Prison alongside Sarah, and our life in the hulks. The long, long voyage and these last two years in Port Jackson.

As if all memory had turned into water, that stream of remembrance flowed over me. But as I clung semiconscious to the cliff face, a woman's voice spoke inside my head. It sounded very much like our own dear mama's voice, though now I wonder if perhaps God was speaking through her? The voice said that I had seen too much, that I had come too far to die in such a forlorn place. The voice commanded me to go on living.

I took a deep breath, and hauled myself up.

Then I was flat on my back, staring up at a sky circling above me. I was looking up at swooping seagulls and fluffy white clouds while the sun burnt a hole in my head.

I closed my eyes and waited for the reddish flashes in front of my eyes to disappear. For the hammering in my ears to stop. For my breathing to slow down.

I must have fallen into a deep slumber. Suddenly Emily was standing right in front of me. She seemed so vibrant and alive, my heart leapt with pleasure at seeing her thus. She beckoned to me, crying that her mama wanted to thank me for looking after her so well. I told her how pleased I was to see her this happy. But then I added, "How can I go with you? You are dead and I am still alive. Besides," I added as she was about to protest, "my own mama tells me that I must stay here."

"Then we will wait for the right time to be together," she promised, and with that she kissed me and I woke up.

I lay there musing over my dream. Emily seemed so content, as did our own dear mama. Could these spirits really have spoken to me? Then I decided that even if these were just figments of my imagination, that I should tell Winston some of this. Might this not comfort him a little?

Wednesday, 2nd June

After I confessed yesterday's mishap, my Master was more upset that I might have drowned or fallen to my death than at the loss of the bucket and knife. We have eaten all our rations. I have nothing to prepare for tonight's meal. But my Master has promised me that he will bring home some vegetables. He says that one of the convicts has an abscessed leg. My Master has promised to lance it for him. Though the wound contains a lot of pus (and this suggests it will get better of its own accord), the convict has pledged some potatoes and carrots in return.

I have yet to talk to Winston. He stays on duty at the barracks until tomorrow. Perchance I will tell him about yesterday's dream. Was my hearing Mama's voice and seeing little Emily just visions? Either way, I know that Emily is far happier now than when she was alive.

I have more fire in me today. I have managed to sweep and dust the hut, and collect more water and firewood. I have even dug over my vegetable patch. My seeds have started to sprout tiny green shoots. Now I must nourish the bed the way our papa and mama did back home. Perchance I will find some horse-droppings near the barracks.

In the late afternoon, I walked as far as Governor Phillip's house. There was the usual group waiting to speak with him. They were quarrelling so much I could hear them as I was coming down the track. Truly it is a great man who can manage such an unruly bunch of officers, seamen and convicts. They say that the Governor has a very stubborn spirit, that he lacks the necessary grace to become a great gentleman, but I think that it is rare to find a ruler who is so impartial. He has even handed over his private stock of flour to be shared around the colony.

My Master tells me that he heard Governor Phillip insist that we would not starve. "As soon as the first ship from England arrives," he promises, "our present sufferings will be over." I pray that he is right.

When I got home, both Winston and my Master were waiting for me. My Master said, "Look at what I have brought for you, Scheherazade. Potatoes and carrots for our supper. But first," he pulled out a bench for me to sit on, "we have something to tell you."

Heart in my mouth – for I expect all tidings to be bad – I waited to hear him out.

He settled on a stool in front of me and said, "Winston and I have been given orders to return to England on the very first ship that sails home."

I took ages to take in what he was saying. Then I wept and wept inconsolably. "What will happen to me now?" I cried at last. "I am not allowed to return before I finish my sentence."

My Master took my hand in both his large ones. "We have learned to love you as dearly as if you were part of our family. We would trust you with our very lives. And we are sure that you have been transported here most unjustly." His face fell into deeper lines. "But not even Captain Phillip has the power to allow you to return before your sentence is complete."

I wept more loudly. My Master glanced at Winston who stared sadly back. He said, "Lizzie, do you not have a good friend in Rose Hill?"

"Sir, that I do," I said wiping my teary face on my sleeve. "I am sure that Sarah is missing me most sorely. Also, when we were on our way to Sydney Cove, I promised the convict woman, Margaret, that I would teach her and Sarah their letters. I would very much like to keep my word."

"Was not Margaret heavy with child?"

"Indeed she was."

My Master's sigh was heavy. "If the baby should happen to be a girl, ask Margaret to call her Emily."

My eyes filled once again. "Sir, that I will indeed."

My Master sighed. "They will be very pleased to have you back," he decided. So he and Winston waited for me to pull myself together. I did, and then set about preparing potatoes and carrots for our supper.

Thursday, 3rd June

The wind is cold and fierce. Autumn has vanished and winter is now upon us.

My household tasks over, I set off towards the storehouse and my favourite place under some red gums that look out to sea.

I took my quill, ink and book. I had intended writing in my journal. Who should I come upon but Winston? I could see that he had been crying for his cheeks were pale and his eyes swollen and red.

I quickly told him about the vision I had of Emily and how happy she had been. I said, "Perhaps God does indeed look after the innocent," and this seemed to cheer him a little.

"You have been such a true friend," he said to me. "Surely there is something I can do for you in return? I would like to repay you for all you have done for Emily... Nay, what you have done for all my family."

There was a long silence as I considered his offer.

"Indeed there is," I replied at last. "You will shortly be returning to England..."

"Only if a ship ever arrives to take us home."

"One must come sooner or later," I said firmly, for I refuse to believe that we have been left here to slowly rot and die.

He pulled a face. "I wish I had your hopefulness of spirit."

"Winston, my favour is this…" I took a deep breath and held up this journal. "Do you recall my reasons for wanting this from you?"

He nodded, but his eyes flickered and I could see that he did not.

I said, "I would dearly like for you to travel to the west of England. Then to go to the Cotswolds and find the village of Cranham. And once you are there to seek out my brother Edward and then to give this book to him."

To my delight and relief he promised to do just this, saying, "I will never forget how much Emily enjoyed the onions you so bravely stole for me. I also admired how much you were prepared to risk so you could write to your brother. You can be sure that this journal will arrive most safely in his hands…"

He was about to say more, when something on the horizon caught his eye. At the very same moment we both heard the echoing boom of a cannon going off.

We jumped to our feet, both shouting with joy. A cannon boom meant that a sail had been sighted. The Second Fleet had finally arrived!

The Second Fleet was sailing into Sydney Cove.

Now we are saved…

Edward, I write this a little later. You cannot imagine what rejoicing there is in Sydney Cove. But all I can think is … now this journal will come to you. Now you will know that I am still alive, that I have never forgotten you and that God willing, one day we will be together again.

Historical Note

This imaginary diary is partly based on the real life story of Elizabeth Hayward. She was the youngest female convict to sail on the First Fleet's transport ship – the *Lady Penrhyn*. On 18th December 1786, Elizabeth was sent to prison for stealing clothes worth seven shillings. She was sentenced in January 1787 to seven years' transportation.

But this is where this diary turns to fiction. The real Elizabeth Hayward was given thirty lashes for insolence in 1788. She was transported to Norfolk Island in March 1790 where she gave birth to at least four children. In 1813 she left the island as the wife of Joseph Lowe. It may be her name on the records of St John's in Launceton: "Elizabeth Lowe who died in October 1836 aged sixty-six."

Two centuries ago many people in Britain lived every day with hunger, dirt, disease and poverty – mainly in cities like London. Streets were choked with rubbish and people lived in crumbling tenement buildings (large blocks of flats). Children from poor families were sent out to work, sometimes when they were just six, and often in life-threatening jobs such as cleaning chimneys or working in the mines. If these children were orphans, they could be bought and sold like slaves.

Crime was widespread in these areas because conditions were so poor – people had to do what they could to survive. There was no central police force, and punishments were often far too harsh for the crime committed. Though many were sentenced to death on the gallows for housebreaking, stealing food or maybe even "fortune telling", many were pardoned by the king and sent to prison instead.

The privately-run prisons were dark and smelly – prisoners even had to buy their own food and bedding. Cells were hardly ever cleaned and, like the city itself, had no proper sewerage system. Many prisoners died of starvation. Prison fever (which we now know as typhus or typhoid fever), swept through the cells.

Another punishment was transportation to America to work on the cotton plantations. But in 1766 the American colonies declared independence from Britain. Prisoners now had to be kept at home in the overcrowded prisons. One solution to this was to strip old ships of their rigging and masts and turn them into "hulks" – massive prison ships. But conditions in the hulks were worse than the prisons. So the government had to look elsewhere – and settled on sending prisoners to Australia.

The English had been interested in finding a base in the Pacific Ocean, and wanted to occupy Australia before the French got there. Captain James Cook had brought back good reports of this great Southern Land – its plentiful timber and flax were perfect for ship building. And so the idea of the First Fleet was born – eleven great ships would take 759 convicts, Royal Marine guards, some officers and their supplies to Australia – with Captain Arthur Phillip as head of the fleet for the long and complicated journey. The ships arrived in Portsmouth on the 16th March 1787 – but the departure was held up. Some convicts were on board for seven months before an outbreak of prison fever hurried things along.

The First Fleet left England on 13th May 1787. They stopped at Tenerife and Rio de Janeiro to get food supplies and send the sick ashore. Because Captain Phillip had supplied oranges and other fresh produce, very few convicts died of scurvy during the voyage compared to later convict fleets.

The First Fleet arrived at Botany Bay between 18th and 20th January 1788. This location had been recommended by Captain Cook in 1770 as a possible place to settle. But the area lacked enough fresh water, was not safe for ships and the soil was far too poor for growing crops. So Captain Phillip sailed north and arrived at Port Jackson on 26th January 1788.

The settlement was to have many problems. Most of the convicts had come from cities and knew nothing about growing their own food or looking after livestock. It was a hot, dry, infertile country – and soon everyone from convicts to Captain were placed on rations.

Before 1788 about 300,000 Aborigines lived in Australia. For more than 30,000 years, these nomadic people had seen very few Europeans – and until 1788 they were probably happier and healthier than most Europeans. They fished and gathered oysters in the sheltered bays. Their lives were rich in story telling, music and ceremonies. Although Governor Phillip tried to befriend the local Iora tribe, their cultures were just too different – and soon the Aborigines and the settlers learned to distrust each other. Diseases like cholera, smallpox and influenza swept through the Aborigine population, killing many and dislocating those that survived.

The Aborigines lived on local plants and fish, but the settlers did not find these appetising. They occasionally ate rats, dogs, possums and kangaroos, but they had little ammunition to hunt with, and they proved to be poor fishermen. Most of the settlers' food had to come from the supplies brought with them on the ships. This resulted in their total dependence on the shipping trade – which did not include Australia on its route. Shelter was also a problem as they didn't have proper tools to build with. They also had very little clothing, and by the time the Second Fleet arrived, convicts and marines alike were dressed in patched threadbare clothing. So things really were desperate for the settlers at the beginning – and some attempted to escape, even though punishments would have been severe if they were caught.

Locations with far better conditions than Sydney Cove had been found by First Fleet ships. Norfolk Island was more fertile, and creatures such as green turtles and mutton birds were used to supplement the Sydney colony's dwindling food supplies. However, the island was surrounded by rocky cliffs which meant that timber could not be loaded onto ships for transport back to Sydney Cove. Exploring the country to the west of the Cove, the settlers found more fertile land on the Parramatta River – a settlement they named Rose Hill. There they soon produced good crops of maize, wheat, barley, oats and potatoes but lack of transport again proved to be a problem.

For the early settlers, the struggle to keep themselves alive was momentous. They started to build on the rocks – the craggy sandstone on the western side of Sydney Cove. Cottages clung to the stone and some dipped dangerously towards the sea. The coast had been stripped of trees and rock to provide ballast for ships, and this gave it a run-down look. If you had been there at the time, you would have been horrified by the smell of rotting waste by the banks of the Tank Stream, and bits of drying flesh from corpses on Gallows Hill. But although Australia was a wild and lonely place, there were no man-eating animals, the climate was hot in summer and mild in winter and it was a healthy country for people, animals and plants. During the 'starvation years' more babies were born and fewer children died than if these early settlers had stayed in England. Forty-five children arrived with the First Fleet. By the middle of 1790, 83 babies had been born – though 25 of the original children had died – (this number of deaths was not considered that high for the time). In 1789

Isabella Rosson established the first school.

Some of the convicts eventually became wealthy and respected citizens. The opportunity of starting afresh in a new land helped many discard their pasts and prosper.

This fictional diary takes place during a two-month period, at a time of great struggle and starvation, when after a series of delays and disasters, the colony was desperately waiting for further supplies to arrive on the Second Fleet.

Timeline

1606 The earliest recorded contact between European and Aboriginal people. A Dutch ship lands on the western coast of Cape York Peninsula.

1642 Dutchman Abel Tasman reaches southwestern Tasmania and claims the territory for Holland, calling it Van Diemen's Land.

1760 King George III becomes king of England. (His reign lasts for 60 years.)

1770 Captain James Cook claims possession of the whole of the East Coast of Australia – raising the British flag at Possession Island off the northern tip of Cape York Peninsula.

1776 The United States of America declares independence from Britain. Britain must find another place to send its convicts.

1787 The First Fleet leaves England on May 13 and arrives at Sydney Cove between the 18th and 20th January 1788.

1789 Outbreaks of smallpox introduced by the British lead to the death and devastation of the Aboriginal population of Sydney and the surrounding areas.

1790 Ships of the Second Fleet arrive at Port Jackson. On the voyage from England, 267 convicts die.

1791 Tobacco is first grown in Australia, citrus trees are planted along the Parramatta River and whaling first begins off the coast of Australia.

The ships of the Third Fleet arrive.

1792 France is declared a republic.

1792 The first free immigrants in Australia settle at Liberty Plains.

1796 Around this time, a naval dockyard is established at Sydney Cove.

1798 Steam-powered spinning begins in English Mills. Workers are replaced by machines.

1799 The beginning of a six-year period of resistance to white settlement by Aborigines in the Hawkesbury and Parramatta areas – known as "The Black War".

1800 The Irish Parliament passes the Act of Union with England.

1802 Matthew Flinders circumnavigates Australia.

1803 The first settlement in Van Diemen's Land (Tasmania).

1803 Australia's first newspaper – The Sydney Gazette and New South Wales Advertiser is founded. First record of a cricket match played in Australia.

1804 The slaughter of Aborigines in Van Diemen's

Land begins. Settlers are authorised to shoot the native people on sight.

1805 The Battle of Trafalgar. The British Navy wins against the French, but lose Admiral, Lord Nelson.

1807 The first Australian wool is exported to Britain.

1807 The slave trade is abolished in the British Empire.

Altogether, between 1788 and 1868, about 137,000 male and 25,000 female convicts were transported to Australia.

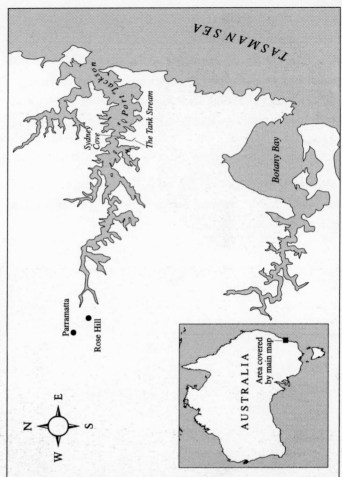

Map showing Australia and the early settlements at Sydney Cove and Rose Hill.

A portrait of Arthur Phillip, the naval commander and Governor of Sydney Cove.

This engraving by a European artist is one of the earliest depictions of native Australian ritual.

A painting showing the ships of the English First Fleet entering Botany Bay in January 1788.

Painting showing prison hulks anchored on the River Thames, London.

An early illustration of a kangaroo drawn during Captain Cook's expedition to Australia in 1770.

Sydney Cove – an illustration of the early days of the colony.

Picture acknowledgments

P 190   Map illustrated by András Bereznay

P 191 (top)   Arthur Phillip, Page, Mary Evans Picture Library

P 191 (bottom)   An Aboriginal gathering, J Neagle, Mary Evans
                     Picture Library

P 192   The First Fleet enters Botany Bay, JR Ashton in
                     Australia Illustrated, Mary Evans Picture Library

P 193 (top)   Prison Hulks, Samuel Prout, Mary Evans Picture
                     Library

P 193 (bottom)   Kangaroos, From Bankes's New System of
                     Geography, Mary Evans Picture library

P 194   Sydney Cove, RF Jukes, Mary Evans picture Library

My Story.

the hunger

The Diary of
Phyllis McCormack, Ireland 1845-1847

10th November, 1845

Horrible! Horrible! The rot has destroyed most of the potatoes which were wholesome and sound when we dug them out of the ground. Da opened up the pit this morning and found it filled with nothing but diseased mush. All we have left to eat are those that hadn't yet gone underground.

"Six months provisions are a mass of stinking rottenness. Where has it come from?" Da kept repeating all morning. "Disease will take us all," he drawled.

My Story.

VOYAGE ON THE GREAT TITANIC

The Diary of
Margaret Anne Brady, 1912

Monday 15th April, 1912

It was after midnight, and I could still hear people moving about in the passageway. Before I had time to go out and join them, there was a sharp knock on my door.

I opened it to see Robert. His eyes looked urgent.

"Good evening, Miss Brady," he said. "You need to put on something warm, and report to the Boat Deck with your life belt."

Miss Brady? When I heard that, I felt alarmed for the first time. "A routine drill," he said. "No need to fret."

I knew he needed to get on with his duties, so I found a smile for him and nodded...

"You'll not want to take your time, Margaret," he said in a very quiet voice.

It did not seem possible, but maybe this was not a drill.

My Story.

BLITZ

The Diary of
Edie Benson, London 1940-1941

Friday 30th August, 1940

Last night was very still and clear. As Dad went
out for the evening shift, he looked up and said grimly,
"If they're ever going to come, it'll be on a night like this."
And sure enough, the first air-raid warning came at a
few minutes past nine. Mum was out at the ARP post,
and Shirl, Tom and I were huddled together in the
shelter with Chamberlain.

Shirl's teeth were chattering already. "Cor blimey!"
she said. "What's it going to be like in the middle
of winter? I've got no feeling in my toes at all."

I could see Tom was about to open his mouth and say
something clever when we heard the first explosion,
and then two more following close on the first one...

My Story.

The Crystal Palace

The Diary of

Lily Hicks, London 1850-1851

17th April, 1850

The Crystal Palace is more wonderful every time we go,
with coloured light everywhere, so airy and delicate, but
strong. Not like a house, solid and heavy and shadowy,
solid to the ground. Like being inside a diamond it is,
or a fairy palace. Master has made a miracle,
everybody says so. And as for the exhibits inside, there
are more and more every day, 10,000 they say. We saw
French and Belgian lace and English embroidery today,
so fine the Queen can't have better – shawls and baby
gowns and waistcoats, and Irish double damask
tablecloths with shimmering ferns and flowers woven in.
I was near crying with pure delight it was all so lovely.

My Story.

TWENTIETH~ CENTURY GIRL

The Diary of
Flora Bonnington, London 1899-1900

22nd December, 1899

Time is marching forward, carrying us over the
threshold and pitching us, willy nilly, into a new
century. The prospect of growing up in that unexplored
territory is so thrilling that I fancy, if I close my
eyes tight, I can almost see the process taking place!
A day slips away like sand in a sand glass and then
another day dawns and so we are caught up in this
inevitable passage towards 1900. I bought a journal
and have begun to transfer all my scribblings of the last
few days into it. It will record my journey into the new
century. I shall call it "Twentieth-Century Girl",
for that is what I intend to be!

My Story.

My
Tudor Queen

The Diary of
Eva De Puebla, London 1501-1513

4th November, 1501

I hardly like to make a mark on the beautiful,
blank pages of this book, but I must. Mama gave it
to me as a parting present so that I could write about
this journey from Spain to England. "Don't waste it,"
she said. "Just write the important things." I'm sure
Mama would be impressed by the great procession in
which we have slowly made our way from the West
Country to London. Horses and carriages, litters and
baggage-waggons and attendants, soldiers, courtiers,
ladies, pages, jesters – and Catherine herself,
Catherine of Aragon on her way to wed Prince Arthur,
eldest son of the king of England.

My Story.

The '45 Rising

The Diary of
Euphemia Grant, Scotland 1745-1746

17th September, 1745

Highlanders shoved a path thro' the crowd all grinning
and cheerful. Pipers followed them, playing "The King
shall enjoy his own again" and then came Prince Charles
riding a white horse. He's incredible handsome. Wore a
white wig, a tartan coat with gold braid and lace at the
neck and cuffs, and a blue sash over his shoulder. The
crowd were cheering, laughing, weeping and shouting,
"Good luck to the Prince!
God bless ye, sire!" Then came streams more
Highlanders, bristling with weapons – scabbardless
swords, pistols and muskets, pitchforks, even cudgels.
Most exciting day of my life – so far!

My Story.

The Great Plague

The Diary of
Alice Paynton, London 1665-1666

July 3rd 1665

Aunt Nell came home from the market looking very pale. She overheard two men discussing the Weekly Bills of Mortality. It seems that in the past week 700 people have died from the plague. So the plague is well and truly come to London after all. After much discussion I am to be sent to Woolwich with Aunt Nell. I refused to go without Poppet and Papa has relented. I was sent to enquire of a carrier but was soon stopped in my tracks. One of the houses in the next street had a red cross painted on the door. Above the cross someone had chalked "Lord Have Mercy Upon Us".

Featuring young men at the centre of each story, this brand-new series covers significant conflicts in world history.

Civil War
Thomas Adamson
England 1643-1650

Trafalgar
James Grant
HMS Norseman 1799-1806

The Trenches
Billy Stevens
The Western Front 1914-1918

Battle of Britain
Harry Woods
England 1939-1941